D1015140

A
NEW
DEMOCRACY

A
NEW
DEMOCRACY

—◆—

By Gary Hart

WILLIAM MORROW AND COMPANY, INC.

NEW YORK   1983

Some of the material in this book first appeared in
The New York Times Magazine on February 14,
1982.

Library of Congress Cataloging in Publication Data

Hart, Gary, 1937-
    A New Democracy

    Includes index.
    1. United States—Economic conditions—1971-
2. United States—Economic policy—1981-
I. Title.
HC106.8.H365   1983b   338.973   82-25912
ISBN: 0-688-01628-6
ISBN: 0-688-01629-4(pbk.)

Printed in the United States of America

First Edition

1 2 3 4 5 6 7 8 9 10

CONTENTS

Introduction: "Unanimity About the New"   7

Part I: The Path to Prosperity   17

    Shaping a Better Future   19
    Foundation for Growth   27
    Restoring Industrial Vitality   46
    A New Employment Strategy   83

Part II: National Security Today and Tomorrow   119

    Perspective on a Changing World   121
    Toward a More Effective Defense   125
    Achieving Energy Security   141
    Preventing Nuclear Holocaust   157

Conclusion   177

Index   178

For Andrea and John

E a special thanks to Donna Rice

ACKNOWLEDGMENTS

The British novelist Laurence Sterne once noted that "writing, when properly managed, is but a different name for conversation." The writing of *A New Democracy* bears out that aphorism. Its publication would not have been possible without the ideas, counsel, and guidance of many people. I am fortunate to have had the assistance of many friends and experts—who offered their knowledge, wisdom, and understanding—over the two years in which I have worked on this book.

I am especially grateful to Kathy Bushkin, whose ideas and insights through the months of preparation of these materials were invaluable, and to Alfred Friendly, Jr., and Timothy Bannon for their help in the tedious task of editing and organizing these thoughts. I am also grateful for the wisdom of the following people. Although my name appears on the jacket of this book, and I am uniquely responsible for its contents, their views were invaluable in its preparation: Alvin L. Alm, Norman Rockefeller Angell, Mayor Marion Barry, Jr., Robert A. Belanger, Samuel R. Berger, Robert Black, Dr. Coit Blacker, Dr. Barry Blechman, Barry Bluestone, Dr. Kingman Brewster, Dorothy V. Brodie, Benjamin Brown, Arthur A. Bushkin, Ron W. Cattany, William V. Chandler, Willard R. Chappell, Pat Choate, Kenneth H. Cholerton, Dorman Commons, Peter F. Cowhey, Dr. Edwin Deagle, Dr. Sidney Drell, Peter Edelman, Barry J. Eichengreen, Representative Geraldine Ferraro, Stephen J. Flanagan, Jay W. Forrester, Stephen J. Friedman, Merrick B. Garland, Karl Gawell, Don L. Gevirtz, Keith Glazer, Peter F. Gold, Professor Robert J. Gordon, Otis L. Graham, Mark Green, Robert Hamrin, Lloyd Hand, Sidney Harman, Willis W. Harman, Denis A. Hayes, Professor Walter H. Heller, Steven Hitchner, John D. Holum, Kent Hughes, Eliot Janeway, Jerry J. Jasinowski, DeWitt John, Terry Johnson, Professor Alfred E. Kahn, Roger Kahn, Carolyn T. Kamlet, Henry Kelly, Irvin M. Kipnes, Harold J. Kwalwasser, Robert S. Lackner, Jonathan Lash, William S. Lin, Martin Lobel, Amory B. Lovins, John T. McEvoy, Robert McIntyre, Ira Magaziner, Hans Mark, Guy R. Martin, Joseph Minarik, David Moulton, John Musser, Professor William D. Nordhaus, William Norris, Sharon Parker, Monte Pascoe, Professor Joseph A. Pechman, Dr. William Perry, Marion W. Pines, Steve Pomerance, William B. Quandt, Perry D. Quick, Baldwin Ranson, Professor Robert Reich, Pat Reuss, Stephen C. Saunders, William Schroer, William Schweke, Tom Scoville, Malcolm B. Seawall, Larry Seidman, Ronald K. Shelp, Alexander W. Sierck, Donald Smith, Larry Smith, Peter J. Solomon, Robert Solow, Thomas Stern, Martin Stone, Charles S. Struckmeyer, Emil Sunley, Professor Stanley Surrey, Kenneth W. Thompson, Professor Lester C. Thurow, Roger Vaughan, Lee Webb, Alan M. Webber, Frank Weil, James Wetzler, Robert H. Williams, Professor Daniel Yergin.

INTRODUCTION "UNANIMITY ABOUT THE NEW"

———◆———

*If we open a quarrel between
the past and the present—
we shall find that we have
lost the future.*

—WINSTON CHURCHILL

America's character is being tested in the 1980s.

Out of this period of testing, we will find out who we are and what we are made of. We will overcome these tests. And by doing so, we will strengthen our national character.

But to prevail, we must maintain our commitments to equal rights and opportunities, to real progress and change in the standard of living and quality of life for our people. We must continue to demand justice. And we must offer promise and hope—for our young people, our unemployed, our poor, our disadvantaged, our elderly.

Our present test is real, and it must be overcome if democracy is to prevail. Its cause is clear. The seemingly natural progression of economic growth and prosperity—and therefore hope and promise—came to a halt in the 1970s. Some of the programs and policies that had fostered this prosperity for more than thirty years ceased to work.

The declining effectiveness of past policies created a vacuum of ideas and leadership now being filled by policies of the Reagan Administration—policies consciously designed to reopen all the old public debates and divisions of the past.

The philosophy of our current Administration is to substitute individual "kindness" for social justice, and private charity for economic opportunity and fairness. It is a policy designed to substitute, for as long as possible, social and economic Darwinism and laissez faire ideology for 200 years of democratically honed egalitarian principles.

A policy of relying on state and local governments for social equity is simply a rhetorical smoke screen. It is an abandonment of national commitment and an erosion of national character. Whatever President Reagan says—and whatever he believes—his policies are dividing this nation. The real test of political leadership is whether it provides confidence and hope, unity of purpose, a sense of commonwealth. The result of this President's policies is to resurrect class conflict in this society for the first time in fifty years.

The test of America's character in this generation is moral, not economic—ethical, not political. Upon the outcome of this test will rest our ability to govern ourselves and our authority to lead the world.

If we wish to preserve and to protect our traditional principles and values, we must find *new* ways to realize them. In an age as troubled as ours, this new agenda must amount to nothing less than a vision for our future that incorporates the noblest values from America's past. For, as the proverb says, "where there is no vision, the people perish."

We should welcome, not avoid, this challenge. For, like similar transition periods in the past, ours is an age of great promise and great opportunity. John Buchan, in his brilliant book *Montrose,* described early-seventeenth-century England thus: "The old world was crumbling, and there was no unanimity about the new."

Because the old world is crumbling under the impact of change, America will decide very soon whether we will move forward or stand still. Indeed, we are making that decision even today in a thousand small ways. We simply lack national leadership capable of putting those many isolated decisions into a coherent framework—of creating "unanimity about the new."

During the remainder of this century, America must re-create its revolutionary and pioneering spirit. Using old-fashioned common sense and American ingenuity, we must devise bold strategies rooted in our basic values and have the courage to carry them out. What is called for is an exercise in government at its best.

Americans still value independence and individuality, as my ancestors in the West particularly did. But we also remember— from frontier times—that common problems can only be solved by people getting together, thinking things through, then deciding how best to act for the common good. That is essentially how this great nation was formed and how it has prospered for two centuries.

The challenge we face today—both our political system and the political parties within that system—is to adapt to enormous change at home and abroad by devising new solutions to sustain old principles.

Our political process began to founder in the late 1970s and early 1980s on the dangerous reef of irrelevance. This period of one-term presidencies, decreasing voter turnout, confused directions, and increased factionalism is not accidental. It is the product of the fundamental failure of our system to deal with change.

It is fashionable to say this is the result of the failure of political leadership. And there is something to that. But political leadership, in a time of transition particularly, requires personal principles and values and the willingness to stand on them.

When I first ran for the United States Senate in 1974, the Watergate scandal was unfolding. It made me, like most other Americans, angry and frustrated. Frustrated because I had first become involved in politics in 1960, during John F. Kennedy's presidential campaign, for very idealistic reasons. I believed government was a positive force to solve problems, that the country needed to activate itself, and that public service was a worthwhile—even noble—occupation. Then, during my first effort to achieve public office, we were confronted with a national political scandal.

In my own case, this experience caused me to start rereading the Founding Fathers, particularly Thomas Jefferson. I wanted to remember—possibly recapture—why this country was founded and what it was supposed to stand for. I couldn't ask people to trust the system and vote for me, during this period when the political system seemed so corrupt, without being able to state clearly my basic political convictions and principles.

Out of this experience came a renewed conviction that I, as a Democrat, wanted to participate actively in the political process because I believed:

- that this nation exists for all individuals, not just the wealthy or the elite.
- that the primary motivation of our society ought to be justice, not personal greed.
- that special privilege and influence are to be resisted.
- that power belongs to the many, not the few.
- that too much power concentrated in the hands of too few people, whether in the private or the public sector, is a threat to individual freedom.
- that our government's constitutional mandate to provide for the general welfare gives it broad powers and responsibilities to promote humanitarian goals and to create an equitable society.

But of all the values these noble principles represent, none is as central to our beliefs as the idea of justice.

The litmus test of justice in a democratic society is equality—

both equality of rights and equality of opportunity. We have more to do on both counts before true justice is realized.

Our nation still must fulfill its promise of equal rights for all. Our Constitution still does not afford equal rights for women as well as for men. Even an agency of the current Administration concedes that job discrimination still exists "virtually everywhere, at every age level, at every education level, at every skill level." Minorities still are discouraged from exercising their basic right to vote.

Our society has yet to offer all its citizens equality of opportunity—a fair chance for both economic advancement and the "pursuit of happiness" promised by our Declaration of Independence. Our tax system provides relief to the wealthy at the expense of the rest of us. The poor, the uneducated, minorities, and women have inadequate opportunities to earn just compensation. Those born in poverty are too likely to die in infancy or to have insufficient health care later in life. Those living in inner cities and suburbs cannot walk through their neighborhoods at night without fear of crime. Those living in congested cities or near factories do not have clean air to breathe.

In the 1980s, we have miles to go to fulfill our national promise that the United States exists equally for all people—for the impoverished as well as the wealthy, for the disadvantaged as well as the fortunate, for the powerless as well as the influential. Government, at its best, is the instrument to realize these fundamental values of compassion and fairness in our society. But increasingly, beyond the traditional question of the role of government in achieving our goals, people are asking, "Where are we going? What *are* the long-term goals? What kind of world are we going to pass on to our children?"

For it is with our children—the common human bond—that our vision must begin. Each of us wants to pass on a better world—a safer, cleaner world with even greater opportunity. This goal unites us all, of whatever race, nation, or ideology.

In the 1980s, to create that vision we must recapture a sense of shared purpose and common interest, uniting as equal participants in one national enterprise. We also must unite with other nations in seeking international solutions to mankind's common problems—particularly a mindless arms race and worldwide recession.

To unite Americans and lead the world, we must understand the enormous changes transforming our lives. The world has always been in transition. Today, though, change is coming faster than ever before, and an increasing qualification of leadership is keeping abreast of our changing age. Any leader who thinks today's world is the same as yesterday's will miss the future.

Consider how much the United States has changed in the past few decades. In 1937, the year I was born, the average family income was $1,346, about 6 percent of today's. In that same year, the gross national product (GNP) was $90.4 billion, less than half the national deficit expected in 1983; the total national budget was $7.7 billion, less than the cost today of a single aircraft-carrier task force.

Change has come even more rapidly in recent years. During the 1962 Cuban missile crisis, the Soviet Union had 75 strategic missiles carrying 75 nuclear warheads; today our two nations together have more than 4,000 of these missiles carrying over 13,000 warheads. Twenty years ago, there were 522,000 steelworkers; today there are only 340,000, and more people work for the McDonald's fast-food chain than U.S. Steel. The first home computer was developed in 1976; about 5 million homes will have them in another two or three years.

Inevitably, as our life changes, our problems change, and our answers must be new.

Our economic challenges are new. For decades, American prosperity was built on our massive industrial base and a bountiful domestic market. Now older industries require new technology to compete, new industries are creating new opportunities for growth, and we are engaged in a world economy.

Our energy challenges are new. For a century, America

could count on vast, cheap supplies of energy to fuel economic growth. Now we know those resources are finite, and foreign sources are dangerously insecure.

Our military challenges are new. In the past, we defeated our enemies by overpowering them with the vast might of our industry and population, outproducing them in tanks, ships, planes, and fighting men. Now we face an opponent with greater military manpower and matériel.

Our security challenges are new. Through most of our history, we were protected by the happenstance of geography. Now our borders can be reached in minutes by nuclear missiles.

But as if to deny this rapid change, too many of our leaders try to force today's problems into the framework of yesterday's world. Much of our public debate is based on false choices, which ensure wrong answers.

We debate whether to revive traditional industries or to encourage new industries, when we should be using technological advances both to rebuild the old and to build the new. We debate whether to make our military "second to none" or to curtail excessive defense spending, when in fact more spending on a military that doesn't work buys us only a larger military that doesn't work. We debate whether to produce more energy for new growth or to conserve energy, when in fact the best opportunities for growth now lie in more efficient use of our finite energy resources.

These outmoded debates are being rendered increasingly irrelevant by a new set of realities emerging in the 1980s and 1990s. They include international economic competition and the resulting domestic industrial dislocation; instability in the international financial community resulting from huge governmental debts; the emergence of an information and service economy; the proliferation of nuclear materials, technologies, and capabilities; increased toxicity in our environment; biogenetic research breakthroughs; global water and land shortages; third-world nationalism; energy supply and price manipulation; and a communications revolution, among others.

A number of Democrats, elected in the 1970s, out of concern for the future course of our party and nation, began to address these new realities in an inventive way—in an attempt to deal with the world as it is, not as it was, and to focus on present and future, not past, problems. These Democrats have attempted to address the new agenda of the 1980s and 1990s while looking outside the established order for ways to make government more compassionate and more fair, as well as more committed to personal freedom and creativity.

The test of our generation and our time will be whether we find new solutions to these new problems based upon our old principles. We cannot go back to the world as it was. The more we care about fulfilling our historic commitment and achieving our traditional values, the more we must adapt to change, the more we must innovate, the more we must create.

Out of our traditional values of social justice and equal opportunity, out of past principles of resistance to concentrated power and insistence on a just government, come the elements of our vision for the future:

- Universal education—as a fundamental promise of democracy, and as the key to our economic future
- A simple, fair, and just tax system—as an obligation of a democratic government to its citizens and as a vehicle for broad-based capital formation
- Industrial modernization—with the President as the principal arbitrator among management, labor, capital sources, and government, of balanced agreements providing an orderly transition to a modern, competitive manufacturing base
- An open trade policy—based upon policies that strengthen all trading partners and liberate United States trade energies in the international marketplace
- Urban modernization—the rebuilding of our national infrastructure through shared federalism, federal capital-expenditure budgeting, and full employment

- A "health for our future" plan—premised upon full health and nutrition programs for *every* American child
- A "frontier" environment—resulting from policies designed to clean up effectively our air and water, to maintain their purity, and to eliminate toxic substances and hazardous wastes from our land
- Energy freedom—liberation from the OPEC stranglehold by wise resource use and careful development of United States energy supplies
- Military reform—designed to provide the world's most modern, flexible conventional forces with weapons that work, officers who can lead, and strategies that are relevant
- Comprehensive nuclear arms control—intensive, immediate, broadly based negotiations led by the United States, involving all nuclear nations, to control—and eventually eliminate—the nuclear threat to human survival

All this is but to suggest, to outline, a vision for today and tomorrow—an agenda to help us resolve our national struggle and ensure the strength of our national character.

No book, no single collection of essays or ideas, can encompass this vast undertaking. But we all must contribute. For, as John Kennedy reminded us, a journey of 1,000 miles begins with a single step. As others contribute their ideas, their goals, their aspirations, taken together, the best of these will guide our nation and light our path.

PART I

---•---

The
Path
to
Prosperity

SHAPING A
BETTER FUTURE

———◆———

Change is the law of life.
Those who live only for the past
or the present are
certain to miss the future.

—JOHN F. KENNEDY

Throughout our history, our nation's goal has been to achieve prosperity and economic security. Each decade since the Great Depression has presented new obstacles to this goal, and the 1980s are no different. But today, more than at any other time since the Depression, traditional economic policies are producing unintended consequences. They are increasingly irrelevant to the unique economic realities of this decade.

Today, we face compound problems: unemployment at disastrous levels, runaway deficits, strangling interest rates, spiraling bankruptcies, idle factories, and diminishing hopes. And beneath the statistics lie countless personal tragedies. For men and women who went from jobs to unemployment lines almost overnight, insecurity has become a new, unwelcome companion. Families have been forced to do without—without the home for which they have saved, the car they need, the college education they

19

hoped for. Optimism has given way to anxiety or even defeat.

As much as each political party may want to point fingers of blame, these problems are only partly the fault of economic mismanagement. During the last several decades, our economy has been undergoing dramatic structural change, a transformation as significant as the Industrial Revolution of the nineteenth century. It is shifting from primary reliance on heavy industry and basic manufacturing to new concentration on advanced technology, information, communications, and services.

At the same time, the United States has increasingly become part of an international economy. We are no longer self-sufficient, nor the undisputed leader. New actors on the world stage influence American economic conditions to a degree that is unprecedented, and to many of us, disquieting.

The task for American leaders in the 1980s is not only to relieve the nation's current distress but also to restore vigorous, sustainable economic growth in drastically new circumstances. The key to our success lies in the creativity with which we adapt our system to master profound changes.

The situation is new in almost all important respects. But while our world has been transformed, we have continued irrelevant debates about the wrong issues. We have argued about false choices: inflation versus recession, the free market versus government control, high technology versus manufacturing, computers versus smokestacks. Important as some people think these questions are, they are not the real choices we face. The patchwork responses they generate provide little present relief and only increase future uncertainty.

We have entered a new economic world, but we act as though we never left the old. We use outdated maps and points of reference, which steer us the wrong way or not at all. And so we miss the reality of our revolutionary times: these times offer far more opportunities than threats.

First, we must not forget that America remains enormously strong, despite stagnation prolonged and aggravated by Reaganomics. The United States has the world's largest economy and domestic market, as well as the highest productivity level, of any nation. Our labor force is highly skilled. Our natural resources are vast. Our scientific and technological advances make us the leader in many fields. Recognizing these strengths, we can assert and build solidly on them.

Second, we have—and need only revive—a clear vision of what we must use our power to achieve. Ours is the only nation ever to have defined the pursuit of happiness as a fundamental right. That first principle remains basic to our nation and our future. We seek growth and a better standard of living for all Americans not because prosperity is an end in itself, but because it furthers humane values—quality and equality.

Finally, we must meet these basic goals not through simple solutions nor sheer power but primarily through creative use of our ingenuity and inventiveness—and by working together. Too many politicians promise instant economic miracles. But no single factor controls our economy, particularly today. Slogans, such as "supply side" economics, are bound to misfire in the future, as they have in the past. The quick fix usually does no lasting good. Only long-term solutions can convert structural revolution into true, positive opportunities.

We must outthink problems, not try to overpower them. The nation that leads the world in the year 2000 will be the one that best develops and harnesses the energies, talents, and ingenuity of its people.

The winds of change are at our back. We cannot resist them. But we can—in a common effort—use them to propel us toward opportunities for greater creativity, toward guarantees of greater security, toward expanded scope for the individual, toward deeper harmonies for the community.

To understand where we should be going, we must look at where we are and how we are changing. These changes are revolutionary. If we gauge their currents correctly, we can deal with them intelligently and harness them creatively.

The Information Revolution

The Information Revolution is both the most familiar and the least well understood of the forces transforming our world. The explosion of innovation in computers, communications, telecommunications, and microelectronics has become the most powerful force for change in the last decades of the twentieth century. More American workers are now engaged in generating, processing, distributing, and analyzing information than are employed in agriculture, mining, construction, and manufacturing goods combined.

We see and experience the change in every facet of our lives—from the automated check-out at the grocery store to our televisions. Twenty years ago every youngster wanted a transistor radio; today, my son has a computer.

Just as the Industrial Revolution dramatically expanded human physical capacities, so the Information Revolution magnifies our mental capabilities. But the new information age does not depend on finite resources such as iron, coal, copper, and oil, which powered the Industrial Revolution; it is driven by our inexhaustible ability to generate knowledge.

In reacting to the Information Revolution, some have tended to stress its dislocations, while others have ignored its opportunities. We must recognize both. Automation, it is true, has meant job loss in many factories and offices. Before the century ends, new machines may change the nature—or perhaps eliminate the existence—of some 45 million traditional jobs. But new jobs are also being created. For every new job in manufacturing between 1970 and 1980, eight new positions were created in the service industries.

Moreover, new technologies can and must be used to revitalize our traditional industries. The increasing role that information and information-related technologies will play in the next twenty years cannot be overestimated. But their increase is not necessarily at the expense of traditional manufacturing industries, such as automobiles and steel. Those industries must again be vital elements of the American economy. But they must also be revitalized by the introduction of new technologies.

The emergence of high technology and services as leading industries has also made it clear that our economy is not homogeneous. It is composed of at least five separate and relatively autonomous economies: agriculture, manufacturing, energy, high technology, and services. Our several economies do not decline or recover from recessions at equal rates. As a result, the national measurements with which we are familiar—unemployment statistics or GNP growth rates, for instance—give us inaccurate pictures of economic performance. Our ailing basic industries, to use the most obvious example, have needs that differ substantially from those of the more buoyant high-technology and energy sectors.

In the same way, and for the same reasons, the needs of Detroit and Dallas have to be weighed separately and addressed differently. Subeconomies are also, often, regional economies—the healthy Sunbelt standing in contrast to the weakened Midwest, reflecting another aspect of fragmentation that policy makers must recognize before we can act intelligently.

A Transformed Labor Force

Another major change in our economy is the transformation of the labor force. No longer are American job holders and job seekers predominantly married males who head their households, work full time, and produce goods. Now more than half of all adult women are on a payroll. Nearly 70 percent of the women born during the baby boom are in the labor market, and almost half of the women with pre-school-age children are working or looking for work. Moreover, the trend is likely to continue—women are expected to make up fully two thirds of the labor force growth between now and 1990.

Further, our work force will be older on average. Elderly

Americans make up 10 percent of our society today. They will account for 17 percent by 2025, playing an increasingly important role in the labor force as we draw on their knowledge and experience.

And, finally, black and Hispanic Americans and other minorities should and will gain an equal footing on the ladder of opportunity.

While the makeup of the labor force changes markedly, there will be much slower growth in its size over the next ten years. The 2.2 percent annual increase of the 1970s will drop to less than 1 percent by 1990, as the baby boom generation matures and eases the pressure for new job creation.

The End of Isolation

When I was growing up, Americans thought that we could do without other countries or make them do what we wanted. We had just won a war. We were the strongest nation on earth. We expected to dominate the world forever.

But it's not that simple. A number of other nations are now competing for world leadership as well. In particular, three new actors each made a forceful debut on the world stage in the 1970s: Japan emerged as our dominant competitor in world markets; the newly industrializing countries, such as Brazil and Taiwan, are competing seriously with us in our traditional markets and offering new ones; and OPEC threatens our economic prosperity and our foreign policy independence through control over oil supplies.

We have reacted to the change in the cast of international economic actors by seeing ourselves as exposed and invaded. We have not seen that in opening ourselves to the world, we have opened it to us. Looking at imports of oil, steel, cars, and electronic technology, we grieve for the lost innocence of self-sufficiency. But today's economic reality and tomorrow's economic promise prevent a return to economic isolationism.

In the last two decades our trade with the rest of the world has doubled as a percentage of our gross national product. More than 20 percent of our industrial products are exported, and those sales provide the base for one of every six manufacturing jobs. Almost one third of American corporate profits comes from sales or investments abroad, and one out of every three farmland acres produces for markets overseas.

The trade news, however, is not all good. America's share of exports to developing countries dropped from 28.3 to 22.1 percent between 1970 and 1978 (while Japan's rose from 21.8 to 26.1 percent). Imports are battering our domestic manufacturing base. Between 1960 and 1979, the share of the United States market taken by American-made cars dropped from 95 to 60 percent; shoes decreased from 98 to 63 percent; textile machinery from 93 to 55 percent; and calculators, adding machines, radios, and television sets from 95 to about 50 percent. We now buy from other nations 14 percent of our steel, 28 percent of the machine tools we use in forming metal, and 90 percent of our cutlery. The statistics explain the clamor raised by business and labor in many industries for higher, stronger barriers against outside competitors.

Economic interdependence—the new reality we have been slow to understand—means more than the loss of complete sovereignty over our own economy. It means also that others must rely on us as both a market and a supplier. On one level, the decisions of OPEC oil producers affect us profoundly without our control. But on another level it means that we can shape the changing world order to our advantage—if we are willing to change our own attitudes and use our enormous strength to project, not to protect, our interests.

An Agenda for Managing Change

There are three key areas for action: the balancing of the monetary and fiscal policies of the federal government; the restoration of

industrial health by modernizing traditional industries and stimulating new growth industries; and the mobilization and full use of
our most important resource—people. All require us to undertake
an economic strategy based upon a common national purpose. The
proposals suggested here are rooted in the economic realities of
today but aimed at anticipating tomorrow's challenges.

This is a full agenda. Importantly, it is a national economic
agenda, not a federal government economic agenda. The challenges before us are far too great and complex for government
policies alone to solve. America must rely on the initiatives of the
private sector, the cooperation of business and labor, and the
strengths of state and local government.

But in a progressive society, the national government must
serve as the ultimate guarantor of social justice and equal opportunity. It should create an economic environment in which the
maximum human potential can be achieved through private investment in private pursuits. It can serve as a catalyst for specific
private initiatives, and may participate in cooperative ventures
with private interests, to achieve the common goals of society. It
must serve as the guardian of the interests of all its citizens, not
just the privileged few. It must prevent practices—economic and
otherwise—by the majority or by the powerful that endanger the
rights and liberties of the few or of the disadvantaged. Finally, it
must be prepared to provide a ladder of opportunity for those
citizens who seek it and who are not otherwise benefited by the
prosperity of others.

Most critically, to compete in an economically complex
world, we must once again assert our nation's economic
strengths. For much of its history, this nation was able to stand
apart from world events. More recently, we were able to dominate them. But as the world evolves toward more dispersed economic power, we must once again control our economic future.

America retains real economic strengths. We must appreciate
them, build on them, and assert them to recapture our historical
confidence. We will then again be able to shape our own destiny.

FOUNDATION FOR GROWTH

———◆———

*The test of our progress is not
whether we add more
to the abundance of those who have
too much—it is whether
we provide enough for those
who have too little.*

—FRANKLIN DELANO ROOSEVELT

Resisting change is a waste of time and energy. Shaping it is the real challenge. But to succeed, we need more than a sense of direction. We must also have an economic structure solid enough to contain the forces of change and flexible enough to modify them.

The cornerstones of such a system must be monetary policies that wisely regulate the supply of money and credit, and fiscal (budgetary and tax) policies that allocate national resources and raise revenues sufficient to meet national needs. Both monetary and fiscal policies have to be consistent and steady. Each must complement the other. Under the Reagan Administration, however, they have not only wavered but clashed. The result has been an economic disaster.

Reaganomics failed in several ways. First, it relied almost solely on monetary policy to control inflation. But it did not just slow circulation of money from lenders to consumers and investors—it cut money off. Combined with other forces in our economic cycle and the world's, unnecessarily high interest rates dampened all economic activity, not just inflation. All other economic objectives—especially growth through increased savings and productivity—were left to fiscal policy.

This mismatch of ends and means was unsound in theory and disastrous in practice. The Reagan fiscal program consisted of massive tax cuts, and thus reduced revenues, with simultaneous huge increases in military spending, and reductions in government support for all other domestic and human needs—from education and environmental protection to care for infants and the elderly. The principal goal all along was not to reduce deficits but to shift priorities massively. The arithmetic of suffering has added up to huge deficits—far from the balanced budgets the President promised. The large tax cuts did not lead to increased private-sector investment because interest rates were too high to encourage borrowing and demand was stagnant. Interest rates stayed high because the government had to borrow more money than ever to finance huge deficits caused by the tax cuts and the frantic military buildup. And consumer demand, stifled by the prohibitive cost of housing and car loans, for example, slowed drastically, leaving warehouse shelves crowded. Producers were stuck with unsold goods and unwilling to manufacture more or invest for future, increased productivity.

The Reagan Administration all along cloaked its dark agenda—the shift of resources from people to guns—in the rhetoric of "balanced budgets."

Some analysts called the situation temporary, a cyclical recession that would, at least, cure inflation even at a terrible cost in unemployment, lost earnings, lost productivity, and, for millions of Americans, lost hopes. Other, more realistic economists defined the standstill as stagnation—American in origin but global in consequence. Indeed, the Reagan economic package played havoc with the economies of our major trading partners. Most of the industrial world suffered from higher interest rates, higher unemployment, and other adverse economic effects in 1981 and 1982 directly because of the Administration's tight-money policy and resulting sky-high interest rates.

Almost all agreed that monetary policy and fiscal policy, working against each other, had compounded our problems. Too few people at work meant lower tax revenues and higher deficits, in part because of increased payments to the jobless. And even when interest rates began to ease in late 1982, there was little prospect that demand for capital or consumer goods would be strong enough to cut quickly into inventories, put people back to work, and stimulate new, productive investment. Having put the economy—and our people—through the wringer, the Administration had left us dried out—beached.

Real recovery requires several obvious conditions—lower interest rates, increased employment, and steadily reduced budget deficits. To start, monetary and fiscal policies must be made to work in harmony. Our policies must be fair, which they are not; coordinated, which they are not; and stable enough to support a prolonged strategy of growth. The restructuring of policies must begin now.

Getting the Federal Reserve Back on Target

The Federal Reserve Board can focus either on the growth of the money supply or on the level of interest rates. Whichever target it chooses to pursue, the Federal Reserve has a considerable impact on the supply of money and credit to the economy. For nearly three years, beginning in October 1979, the board shifted from its earlier focus on interest rates to the supply of money. That policy represented a historic break from the past practice of attempting to keep interest rates reasonably stable in relation to the pace of inflation. The new emphasis left rates to fluctuate freely. They did, but only in one direction—disastrously upward. The Federal Reserve eased up a bit in late 1982, but not before terrible damage had been done.

It did not have to happen. It must not happen again. To

prevent a recurrence, the Federal Reserve Board should bring its targets into line with the objectives for the economy as a whole. In part, this requires that monetary authorities return to their former focus on the level of interest rates. It also means that the board should be required—as it is not now—to calculate annual targets for the growth of money and credit consistent with the long-term real growth rate of the economy. This boils down to ensuring that our economic growth objectives are assisted, not thwarted, by monetary authorities.

Will Rogers was only exaggerating a little when he joked that there have been "three great inventions since the beginning of time: Fire, the Wheel, and Central Banking." The Federal Reserve is not an "invention" that needs to be scrapped. But we should trim its independence by requiring it to conduct monetary policy in greater harmony with fiscal policy, so both work to achieve noninflationary growth. In 1982, Congress included broad guidelines on monetary policy in its annual budget resolution. Congress should continue this practice while seeking other initiatives.

Priorities for the Budget

The budget must be overhauled. Two years of the Reagan program have thrown it seriously out of balance—in two senses of that word. First, it has created astronomical deficits. Second, it no longer reflects the priorities of our nation.

The budget itself, as Congress considers it, is a dry, mind-glazing compendium (nearly 600 pages long in 1982) of dense tables, large figures, and small print. But the budget, beyond the statistical sum of its parts, is the embodiment of our values as a people. Reaganomics has misread and misplaced these values.

The first three Reagan budgets are powerful testimony to this disruption and distortion. By October 1982:

- 890 school districts had been forced to cut back on special-education activities.
- 150,000 working families had lost their eligibility for government-supported day-care, which enabled them to hold jobs.
- Over 660,000 children had lost Medicaid coverage.
- 3.5 million children, about half from low-income families, had been eliminated from the school lunch program.

Yet the heavy cuts in human potential and economic justice did not reduce the *towering* deficits. The money "saved" was merely shifted to the military programs in the budget, to the Administration's five-year, $1.6-trillion armament spree. Just after resigning as chairman of the Council of Economic Advisers in the summer of 1982, Murray Weidenbaum admitted: "On balance, we really haven't cut the budget. Instead the reductions in spending growth in non-defense areas that Reagan won from Congress have been offset by the growth in defense spending." What was not offset, what guaranteed the deficits that are the companions of the Administration's radical revision of budget priorities, was the heavy loss of revenues from the tax cuts.

Seeing what went wrong, we can also identify what must be put right. Four related efforts are required to achieve a genuinely balanced budget—balanced in revenues and spending, and balanced in placing the appropriate emphasis on national security, protecting and strengthening our human resources, and ensuring future economic vitality. To eliminate unacceptable deficits, we must insist on efficiency in all areas and make investments in some we have neglected.

We must start with the defense budget. It must bear its share of belt tightening—and it can. At least $20 billion in military authorizations could have been eliminated from the 1983 Reagan budget request without any loss in military effectiveness. Similar savings can be obtained in the following years by eliminating weapons too complex to work in combat and by making Pentagon procurement truly cost effective. Without cutting readiness or military pay, we can save money by—among other proposals—replacing the B-1 bomber and two giant aircraft carriers with more effective and affordable alternatives. Congress has approved these weapons systems based on a "credit card" psychology that says we will not have to pay for them this year. But the bills are huge, and they eventually come due.

Our defense focus should be on investment in quality, not just quantity; on buying wisely, not just buying more. And a steady pace of investment in defense makes more sense and provides a stronger foundation for long-range military planning. But, as I will argue later, financial targets are *not* the proper basis for structuring the best national security.

Second, we must be willing to reform and modernize so-called entitlement programs. Politically, these expenditures are the most sensitive, the most sacred in the budget. We must protect past promises and ensure future security—including Social Security, medical programs, pensions, and retirement programs—but at a cost that does not leave us only with the grim choice of higher taxes or higher deficits.

Third, to undo in 1983 the mistake made in 1981, we must eliminate the last scheduled 10 percent personal tax cut, or at least defer it until economic conditions improve. This step will help bring the government's income somewhat closer to balance with its outlays, and, by cutting the deficit, will also reduce the pressure of Treasury borrowing on interest rates. We simply cannot afford the tax cut now—not when it means financing $60 billion in extra debt at high interest. We should also combine action on the scheduled tax cut with tax reforms, closing $15 billion or more in unjustified loopholes.

These measures still will not bring the budget into balance. To close the remaining gap, we must have a vigorous economy, one that generates jobs and revenues. The cost to the government—not counting that to the nation as a whole—is $25 billion to $30 billion in lost revenues and increased benefit payments for every 1 percent of unemployment.

Our fourth priority for action, with those immediate and hidden costs in mind, must be investment to stimulate economic growth. Some programs cut by the Reagan Administration, such as aid to education, must be expanded. Some long-neglected areas must now be made national priorities. To save pennies, Reaganomics sacrificed pounds by reducing investment in job training, education, community development, and research and development. Those false economies hurt deeply. They must be reversed. And years of negligence in maintaining our nation's public facilities—from roads to water systems—must be remedied by a long-term investment program involving all levels of government. Our decaying infrastructure blocks growth. Furthermore, we must invest in people, as well as roads, dams, and cities, to capitalize on human skills and to restore the fabric of our national community. The alternative to repair, investment, and growth is decline and deterioration.

Almost every week in my office I get a chance to talk with Coloradans visiting Washington, and usually I get a double-barreled blast on the budget. The deficit, my constituents and I agree, is way too high. Federal spending has to be cut, the visitors say. But before they leave, they add a second message: please do something to save this program or increase that one, or get us government help for some other activity the state or the community cannot finance.

We obviously cannot have it both ways. But we can restore balance among our budget priorities by forgoing an extravagant tax cut, by exercising restraint and wisdom in defense spending, by reforming entitlement programs, and by putting our money where our future lies—in mobilizing America's people and resources for sustained growth.

Budgeting for the Long Term

Four frustrating years on the Senate Budget Committee have left me convinced that we must change our way of making budgetary decisions. Each year, Congress makes tough choices among direct spending programs which now amount to more than $700 billion. But we never systematically examine a different set of budget figures: tax expenditures of $270 billion. Tax expenditures are incentives, loopholes, or rewards in the tax laws that try to encourage certain preferred behavior. They are not calculated in the budget process. They should be.

We also need a better system on the spending side of the ledger. We should treat the budget as any business—or any family—does, separating the expenses of current operations (salaries, maintenance, short-term supplies, and so forth) from investments that require a multiyear commitment and bring a measurable long-term return (housing, research and development, infrastructure, training). In short, we need a capital investment budget.

We do not have such a system now. Instead, the "unified" budget lumps funds for hospital construction and energy research together with crop support payments, fuel costs for fighter aircraft, and maintenance charges for public buildings and lands. Generally the federal budget allocates the full cost of a capital project over the years of construction. A capital budget would account for such costs over the productive life of the capital asset, and our failure to do so distorts our priorities for capital investment.

Few American families could purchase a house, car, or college education if they could not finance—and distribute—the costs over time. Similarly, few American businesses could invest in research-and-development activities or new plants and equipment if they could not obtain long-term financing. Why, then, should the federal budget have to reflect long-term investments during the few years of construction, rather than as we use them?

Just as the unavailability of long-term financing would lead to serious underinvestment in capital goods by the private sector and put a heavy brake on economic activity, so the lack of a federal capital budget has caused chronic underinvestment in long-term public capital assets. This outdated practice seriously threatens our efforts to revitalize the economy.

America's dams, bridges, streets, and sewers are deteriorating faster than we can replace them. We must spend over $2.5 trillion simply to maintain our infrastructure in its current condition. The additional improvements necessary to sustain a growing economy will cost billions more. Yet, in real dollars, the federal government is investing 35 percent less in public facilities now than it was in 1965.

Some facts illustrate the enormity of the problem:

- One fifth of the nation's bridges require major rehabilitation or reconstruction. The Department of Transportation recently classified 45 percent of them as deficient or obsolete.
- The interstate highway system requires reconstruction of 2,000 miles each year.
- A survey of 6,870 communities found that 3,000 had wastewater treatment facilities operating at over 80 percent of capacity and thus could not accommodate any further industrial expansion.
- The nation's 756 urban areas with populations over 50,000 will need up to $110 billion simply to maintain their water systems over the next twenty years.

The deteriorating national infrastructure could take a large human toll. In Colorado, in the summer of 1982, an eighty-year-old earthen dam burst, killing several campers and flooding the scenic town of Estes Park. A recent Federal Highway Administration study found that spending an extra $4.3 billion to fix dilapidated bridges and roads could prevent 48,000 injuries and save 17,000 lives over fifteen years.

The economic costs of insufficient public investment are equally great. U.S. Steel spends an extra $1 million a year to detour its trucks around a closed bridge in Pittsburgh. An industry group estimates that the aggregate cost to the private sector of bad roads and bridges is $30 billion a year—for everything from broken axles to lost business.

It is more difficult to measure the economic cost of underinvestment by the federal government in human resources—that is, in general education, vocational education, job training, and retraining. Yet, by failing to invest wisely in our people, our greatest national resource, we widen the gap between their skills and our changing economy's urgent new needs. Thus, we threaten both our competitiveness in world markets and our national standard of living.

A federal capital budget, as a component part of a national infrastructure strategy, would begin to reverse years of failed pork barrel politics and *ad hoc* decision making on public investments. It would provide us with the information necessary to weigh competing claims on the federal treasury—such as defense and social programs—and to allocate scarce resources to those investments yielding the greatest benefits for the public.

Capital investment budgeting is not a new approach. It is used by virtually all of America's businesses and over two thirds of the state and local governments, because it provides the only realistic picture of capital needs.

To place capital expenditures in their proper perspective, Congress should enact legislation that would require that the federal budget distinguish between capital investments and operating expenses, and define a capital investment as a budget outlay used for the construction, acquisition, or rehabilitation of an asset with a useful life longer than one year. Capital expenditures would include, among other things, investment in research and development, general and vocational education, job training, and retraining. This would not change government procurement or contracting practices, but it would allow us to account for the costs over the years an investment serves us.

If we could see clearly the difference between capital investment and current expenditure, we could strike a better balance between short-term costs and investments in our future. And we could see clearly where we are shortchanging the future to live better now.

Fighting Inflation Effectively

When 12 million Americans are out of work and factories are operating at less than 70 percent of capacity, it is natural to concentrate on the evils of inducing a recession to combat inflation. But we must also think ahead to eventual economic recovery and the inflationary pressures it will bring.

We do not have to ride the roller coaster of double-digit inflation and double-digit unemployment—if we can find a means to counter the natural momentum of wage and price increases. One such weapon is mandatory government controls, but they are a poor weapon at best. Mandatory controls are a policy of last resort, of enormous cost and little, if any, lasting benefit. They merely contain the problem for a short period of time—a temporary breather before the inevitable explosion when the lid is removed. As a cure for inflation, mandatory wage and price controls may be marginally less painful than the disease, or than the massive unemployment caused by the Reagan Administration's reliance on tight money to fight inflation, but they impose distortions on our system and a vast additional bureaucracy on our government, neither of which is necessary.

A different and promising approach is a tax-based incomes policy (TIP). A TIP uses taxes to encourage, but not require, wage and price restraint. Here's how it would work.

Guidelines would be established for both prices and wages. There would be a single wage standard for the economy and a set of price standards for each major sector of the economy. The wage standard would reflect the average labor productivity growth rate for the whole economy, and the price standards would reflect the average labor productivity growth rate for each individual sector.

If a corporation's price or wage increases exceeded the guidelines, its tax rate would increase by a certain percentage. Thus, firms would be free to raise prices or wages above the guidelines, but would pay a tax penalty for doing so. Such a system could also provide rewards in the form of tax breaks to both companies and workers who held prices and wages below the guidelines.

We've never tried a TIP, although many noted economists have studied the idea extensively. But as the specter of inflation reemerges, it's a plan worth trying before we resort to other, more extreme measures.

A TIP has a number of advantages. The flexibility it would provide is far better suited to American practice than mandatory controls. The tax incentives would be more effective than government jawboning has been as an inducement to restraint. And the policy would give us an alternative to the unemployment disasters of old-line tight-money mechanisms. But its most compelling feature is that it goes right to one of the root causes of inflationary pressures: the price-wage spiral. Indeed, a TIP, complemented by a proper monetary and fiscal policy mix, is the only policy that holds out the prospect of reducing and holding down inflation and unemployment simultaneously.

A TIP has several other advantages that make it worth considering. First, it is market-oriented. It uses an instrument that has proved its effectiveness in our market economy: financial incentives. It leaves business and labor free to make their own decisions without government interference.

Properly administered, a TIP is also fair. It must cover both prices and wages for it to be judged equitable. With such a plan, we can lay to rest, once and for all, the fear that a TIP must be biased against labor. In fact, perhaps the most compelling argument for a TIP is that workers are sure to be worse off without it. Literally millions of workers have borne the heavy cost of prolonged unemployment under the Reagan anti-inflation strategy. Surely it is time to try a fair and flexible alternative that will allow us to focus all our efforts on economic growth.

And this proposal can be administered without extraordinary new costs. It should be limited to the 2,000 largest corporations, which constitute about half of our economy. This would exempt the millions of smaller corporations, partnerships, and proprietorships from any compliance costs. This is a sound feature, for it would make the TIP administratively feasible and inexpensive (the Internal Revenue Service, through its existing corporate tax system, could efficiently monitor the performance of these firms), but would not hurt its effectiveness, as the large firms set the wage-price pattern for the country. Smaller corporations would be obliged to follow the general price-wage patterns set by the big companies in order to remain competitive.

Finally, a TIP does not have to be a permanent program. The law creating it could mandate that it be phased out of existence automatically if and when inflation stabilized.

It may not be the only solution to inflation, but it is clearly worth trying. No one has offered a better idea, a more equitable, more effective, more efficient approach. We have little to lose and a great deal to gain from a TIP experiment.

Taxes: Roads to Reform

Right now we are losing both money and part of our national character because of the inefficiencies and inequities of our current tax system. That system must be reformed. And—although many such attempts have been made before and have gone for nothing—I sense that Americans, at last, have lost patience with political delay and partisan manipulation. The special interests that have so long succeeded in warping the tax code to their benefit are still strong, but they face a new sense of our national interest, a powerful tide of change.

That tide can be directed to produce a new tax system that is fair and simple and efficient in stimulating the forces of the market to work for productive growth. The laws we have meet none of these three standards. Our laws reward the wealthy at the expense of the poor and middle class. They are so complicated that more than half of those who file individual tax returns need professional help in preparing them. And these laws make it worthwhile for the rich to hide their income from taxation in ways that contribute little or nothing to real productivity.

Unjust laws invite evasion. Perhaps the worst effect of an unfair tax system is that it encourages honest Americans not just to dodge the law but to cheat. Where government rests on the consent of the citizens such conduct poisons the society, not just the tax system. We cannot afford such a cost.

The complexity of the income tax code has brought a whole industry into being. By one estimate, Americans spend $64 billion a year on accountants, lawyers, and others who prepare our returns. That sum is more than what we collect in corporate taxes, more than the interest paid on the national debt in 1980, almost half of the discretionary civilian portion of the federal budget. And much of the money is spent on a fundamentally unproductive activity—devising ways to avoid taxes.

The labyrinth of tax provisions has also produced increasing inequity. The central feature of the American income tax used to be its progressivity. It put a proportionally heavier burden on those most able to pay. But that was in the past. The majority of the exemptions and shelters that have been inserted into the law over the years now protect those most able to pay—at the expense of those least able to pay and the middle class. As a result, individuals who earned over $200,000 a year and, before 1982, faced a top rate of 70 percent were actually paying taxes at an effective rate of only 25 percent. In corporate taxation, the picture is even worse. The statutory rate is 46 percent, but nearly half the profitable businesses in our country pay no tax at all. Corporations paid 25 percent of all federal tax revenues in 1960, but only 12 percent in 1980. Reaganomic "reforms" are lowering even that dwindling share.

Finally, on top of wasteful complexity and damaging inequity, our tax system has become staggeringly inefficient. Special statutes favoring various kinds of economic activity have left a jumble of tax rates ranging from 40 percent on some kinds of investments to sharply negative rates on other sheltered income.

These tax privileges have made a shambles of the role the market should play in allocating capital. To take just one example, tax laws making all interest payments deductible have the effect of subsidizing corporate mergers and takeovers, for companies can borrow huge sums to finance ventures that bring nothing new or productive into the economy.

All these faults and more have been widely discussed. But it is now time to stop talking about tax reform and start achieving it. We need more than ritual denunciations and the annual tinkering that has left us today's unworkable hodgepodge of statutes and regulations. We must replace, not just revise, our current system. We must do better than follow the joking jingle that has often seemed our motto: "Don't tax you. Don't tax me. Tax that fellow behind the tree." We must instead have tax laws that raise revenues fairly, simply, and efficiently.

Using those essential criteria, we can discard most of the "flat tax" proposals launched in 1982. They received a great deal of publicity at the time because they were undeniably simple. In that respect, they fed on the same instinctive yearning for a quick fix that had given us the Reagan tax cuts the year before. But like those massive reductions, the flat tax idea is profoundly unfair and therefore doomed.

The simplicity of the proposal was seductive. It would tax all income at the same rate: somewhere between 10 and 20 percent. Seemingly equitable at first glance, such a system would actually have shifted the tax burden even further from the wealthy and placed it exactly where it always seems to end up—on the backs of the middle class.

Some simple arithmetic explodes the idea of fairness in the proposed flat rates. Wealthy taxpayers, defined as those with an annual income of over $100,000, now have an effective tax rate of around 25 percent. To lower that rate, as a flat tax of 10 to 20 percent would do, while continuing to afford some tax protection to the poor, would obviously put the revenue squeeze on middle-class taxpayers. Families earning between $20,000 and $50,000 a year, particularly homeowners, could see their tax bills rise 25 to 50 percent under such a scheme.

The designer of one prominent flat-tax proposal, Robert Hall, has admitted that the 19 percent rate he advocates would *raise* taxes by $1,500 a year for families with an income of $30,000, while *cutting* the payments made by the wealthiest Americans by two thirds or more. Such calculations make it evident that the flat tax, though proposed in the name of simplicity, is really meant as a tax break for the rich. It should not become law, and it will not.

There are two other alternatives that are fairer and deserve consideration instead. Under both most taxpayers would pay no more than they do today. The first is a proposal developed by Senator Bill Bradley and Representative Richard Gephardt, called the fair tax.

This would drop the tax rate to 14 percent for single taxpayers with incomes up to $25,000 and for couples with incomes up to $40,000. A progressive surtax, ranging from 6 to 14 percent, would be applied to incomes above those levels. To make sure we have sufficient revenues from these reduced tax rates, most tax credits, exclusions, and deductions would be eliminated, with the exception of a few claimed over many years by the majority of taxpayers and those needed to alleviate genuine hardship. These are charitable giving, home mortgage interest, some medical expenses, state and local income and property taxes, and Social Security and veterans' benefits. Interest earned on state and municipal general-obligation bonds also would remain tax exempt to facilitate raising revenues for appropriate public purposes.

To ensure fairness for taxpayers at the low end of the income scale, the personal exemption would be increased from the current $1,000 to $1,500, and the zero bracket amount for joint returns would be lifted from the current $3,400 to $4,600.

This fair tax *would* be fair. It would be simple. And, because it would eliminate most deductions, it would also close the loopholes that have made the search for tax shelters such a powerful, distorting force in investment decisions. With lower rates for most taxpayers and a broader taxation base, we could still raise the same amount of revenue.

The fair tax represents an attractive simplification of our current system. But there is another, more dramatic alternative that should also be considered. Specifically designed to stimulate savings and productive investment, this tax would be imposed on income we *spend,* instead of income we *earn.* The proposal is new, but the idea is old. Thomas Hobbes argued for it more than three centuries ago, suggesting that society tax people for what they take out of the economic pie, not what they put in.

Unlike a sales or value-added tax collected at the cash register, this savings-incentive tax would be a progressive annual income tax. Basically, it would require a calculation of total income, the amount of income saved or productively invested, and the difference between the two. That difference—minus a large standard deduction of $10,000 to $15,000 replacing most present itemized deductions—would be the amount taxed at progressive rates.

Besides its relative simplicity, such a system of taxation offers three advantages. First, by encouraging saving and investment at all levels, the reform would contribute to our capital base and productivity. Whether the income put into a savings account or common stock or the start-up of a new business amounted to $1,000 or $100,000, it would be a deduction, not taxed until it was spent. There is no more direct incentive to save. There would, of course, have to be a stiff inheritance tax to prevent the transfer of large amounts of accumulated wealth at death.

Second, by treating all income alike, this reform makes the tax system neutral in relation to investment decisions, instead of meddlesome as it is now. Wages, salaries, and tips—now distinguished as earned income—would be reported just as they are now. But other items presently given special treatment, such as capital gains, depreciation, depletion, amortization, and partial exclusion of annuities, would be placed on the same footing. Unproductive shelters would disappear. Instead of investing primarily for tax advantage, Americans would use their capital to seek the highest potential yield.

Third, this alternative approach to taxation would restore our original commitment to progressivity. Will Rogers was right, not joking, in declaring that "people want *just* taxes more than they want *lower* taxes." We have lost that assurance of equity with the proliferation of loopholes. We must regain it.

Both the fair tax and the savings-incentive tax would mean a marked alteration of our system. Such changes would also bring some serious problems. Any transition from the current code would have to be carefully planned. We would have to consider, for instance, how to treat municipal bonds purchased with the assurance that their income would always be tax free, and we would have to face the need to provide direct federal support to the kinds of community investments such bonds now finance. Under a savings-incentive tax the top marginal rates would have to be higher than the current 50 percent rate. Given a large standard deduction, the highest rates would only apply to consumption by the wealthiest citizens, but such rates could contribute to a potential problem, encouraging the untaxed accumulation of capital and a significant concentration of holdings. Far-reaching gift and estate tax reforms would have to accompany a switch to a savings-incentive tax.

In short, as much as we need major change, we also need to study carefully the changes we make. Americans deserve a tax system they can respect. They also deserve—right now—a thorough debate on the shape that system should take.

A malignant recession (and selective depression) and interest rates made unacceptably high by conscious policy are both the effect and the cause of bankrupt economic theories.

No specific proposal to help workers, to help American industries, or to help a city, state, or region can possibly succeed where wrong-headed ideas and unjust and unfair dogmas have poisoned the economic environment. Without balanced national budget priorities and a dependable, affordable supply of money and credit, a new industrial strategy and a dynamic employment strategy cannot succeed.

Taken together, however, a just allocation of public resources, reasonably available investment capital, and a modern strategy for reshaping our industry and human skills will make this nation the dominant world economic power once again.

RESTORING INDUSTRIAL VITALITY

---◆---

*The competitive industry is not one
for lazy or confused or inefficient men:
they will watch their customers
vanish, their best employees
migrate, their assets dissipate.
It is a splendid place for men of force:
it rewards both hard work
and genius, and it rewards
on a fine and generous scale.*

—GEORGE J. STIGLER
1982 Nobel laureate

American industry is fighting the world and its own past. It is stumbling backward into the future. Without a substantial change in direction our prospects will not improve. But such a shift is possible, as well as urgent.

It must begin with the adoption of a far-sighted industrial strategy, one that gives new strength to the traditional engines of our economic growth and encouragement to the industries breaking new ground. We need to ask ourselves continually what type of industrial structure we should work toward in the year 1990 to ensure a globally competitive position. The Japanese are asking themselves this question, as are the West Germans, the French, and most other developed nations. It is well past time for the United States to begin looking ahead and looking abroad.

For many years, we have been improvising at best. Reacting only to emergencies or special pleading, government assistance has been doled out helter-skelter. A jumble of tax breaks, bailouts, and direct subsidies has left us without long-term guidance or priorities. Old and often complacent sectors of industry have earned the rewards of entrenched power, while innovation has been slighted or frustrated. And as competition from other nations has grown in our own and foreign markets, we have tended to become defensive instead of aggressive. We are losing not inventiveness, but initiative. We have to change course and speed. I believe we can.

In combination with the monetary and fiscal reforms already outlined and the employment goals discussed in the next chapter, we need an industrial strategy that can restore the internal dynamism of our major industries and marshal the abundant resources of business, labor, and government to renew our competitive drive around the world. At the center of this strategy stands the idea that the technological revolution—primarily in information technology and biotechnology—holds vast potential for bringing on an "industrial Renaissance" in American industry.

Throughout our economy—in steel and autos as much as in electronics and biotechnology—the potential for modernization and growth is great. Only the coordination needed to mobilize that potential is lacking. That is the component a genuine, creative industrial strategy must supply.

It should have three broad objectives:

- To make the health and competitiveness of individual industries a primary economic goal

- To establish a coherent framework for government programs affecting those industries
- To instill a cooperative instead of confrontational attitude in business, labor, and government

It is also important to be clear on what an industrial strategy is not. It is not central economic planning, and it is not Japanese-style "picking the winners" or "propping up the losers." Such central government control or direction over our lives is clearly unacceptable.

An American industrial strategy for the future can take many forms, and many experts have proposed widely varying programs. I believe six sets of initiatives, including a new effort by the government to anticipate and help shape the future of our key industries, are required.

First, we need a new process, initiated by the President, to create long-term agreements by management, labor, financial markets, and government designed to help our major industries become more competitive in the changing international economy. In addition, we need to provide increased rewards for entrepreneurs in our society. And we need to make better use of our largest pool of capital—employee pension funds—to achieve a wider variety of economic and social goals. New public and private research-and-development commitments must be made to halt the approaching loss of our world leadership in technological innovation. We need a trade policy for the 1980s, based on aggressive promotion of American exports and creatively managing imports at home. And finally, we must remedy the disjointed and shortsighted approach of the federal government to industrial growth by creating a small council capable of providing long-range vision into the industrial future.

These six imperatives define an agenda of specific actions. They reflect as well the most compelling need of all—the need to change ingrained attitudes about ourselves, our government, and our world.

Quite simply, reality obliges us to think differently about the business we do and the way we do business. We cannot afford to be anything but competitive at home. We cannot afford anything less than a national strategy to rejuvenate our industrial power, and we must begin our efforts by reorienting our thinking to fit our altered circumstances.

Alfred P. Sloan once described Henry Ford as a man who "had had . . . many brilliant insights in [his] earlier years, [but] seemed never to understand how completely the market had changed from the one in which he had made his name and to which he was accustomed. . . . The old master failed to master change."

America—the old master of economic growth and technological dynamism—cannot fail to master change.

Our Current Haphazard Approach

As a nation, we essentially face a choice. We can engage in a battle between competing regions and competing industries for a share of piecemeal federal programs. Or we can try to rise above the unnecessary and divisive "sunrise industry–sunset industry" debate and develop a strategy for encouraging the economic health of the nation as a whole.

That's what we should do—but we're not doing it today.

Today, the United States has not one industrial policy, but dozens. No guiding philosophy unifies them. No consensus about government's role in the marketplace and no strategy of industrial development exist to weld public-sector activities to private energies. Instead, *ad hoc* responses and scattershot intervention have dissipated federal resources. Worse than throwing money at problems, we have too often thrown it at the wrong problems and aggravated others through neglect.

"A billion dollars here, a billion dollars there," the late Senator Everett Dirksen used to say with bitter humor, "and pretty soon you're talking about real money." I am talking about real money—the $304 billion in direct outlays and tax expenditures the federal government spent in industrial assistance in 1980. That sum amounted to nearly 14 percent of our gross national product, but there was no agreement on whether that huge flow of resources helped to power our development or erode our strength. In 1980, for instance, the government:

- provided over $6 billion in loans and loan guarantees to the shipbuilding industry and $940 million in loans and loan guarantees to automobile manufacturing.
- gave out over $5 billion in research and development subsidies for nuclear power but only $942 million for coal.
- made $455 million available in tax breaks for the timber industry but nothing in direct aid for semiconductors.
- spent five times more money on research and development for commercial fisheries than on research into new steel technologies.

Such comparisons measure only a part of the unintended impact of unexamined federal policies. Billions of dollars of industrial adjustment assistance over the past twenty years simply have not been used for their intended purpose. Tax code provisions, for example, made it advantageous for U.S. Steel to buy Marathon Oil, borrowing to finance a merger but not to invest in modernizing its own production facilities. The company's decision, encouraged by government indifference, did nothing to put thousands of jobless steelworkers back to work, nothing to stop the industrial blight from spreading to communities like Youngstown, Ohio, and nothing to make America's steel industry stronger in the face of international competition.

Other special breaks—embraced by the Reagan Administration despite its determination not to interfere with the market—include the creation of All-Savers certificates to assist the savings and loan industry and special depreciation rates favoring railroads, cable television, and oil and gas drilling. Winning voluntary import quotas on automobiles from Japan and restrictions on European steel sales to the United States, the Administration continued the trend of its predecessors, intervention *without* obtaining assurances of long-range modernization and competitiveness.

Such haphazard responses stand in sharp contrast to the generally far-sighted, coordinated, and cooperative approach we have practiced for over 100 years in the agricultural sector. The approach began with land grant colleges in 1862 and continued with extension programs delivering technical and managerial information to individual farms, price supports, and much more. The result is an agricultural sector that is the world's most highly productive and has produced abundant food available to the American people (and people overseas) at reasonable cost. Ironically, it is this very abundance, coupled with recent adverse trends in worldwide demand and foreign agricultural trade practices, that is currently causing great hardship for American farmers. Unprecedented surplus levels have driven down prices while costs continue to rise. The key to American agriculture's world-leading productivity level has been consensus on national policy goals. That consensus must now be reactivated to address the tragic plight of American agriculture. But equally important, the type of cooperative approach followed in the agricultural sector could serve as a model for the development of policies for other sectors, since the basic elements of an effective industrial strategy are all present.

Haphazard responses, whether to real needs or simply to effective political pressure, have failed. Government has a crucial role to play in assisting industrial development in the interest of military as well as economic security. But when Washington meddles instead of thoughtfully organizing its assistance, the result is disorder, misplaced incentives, and waste. We have saddled ourselves with expedients. What we require is a far-sighted strategy.

An affirmative industrial strategy focused on restoring the

vitality of all American industries would have far-reaching consequences: the production of high-quality, competitively priced goods and services attractive to the nations of the world.

Industrial Modernization and Growth Agreements

A national strategy for industrial revitalization requires first that we address the needs of our traditional industries, which must regain their competitiveness in the world. We cannot expect to have a stable economy or regain world leadership without modern, competitive steel, auto, textile, and other manufacturing industries.

This goal must be pursued at the highest level of government—by the President. The prestige and persuasive power of the presidency must be engaged in an intensive effort to reach agreements on modernization and growth in our major ailing industries. These compacts would cover commitments by management to long-term levels of employment and worker retraining. They would commit labor to easing the introduction of new technologies. And they would identify the public and private sources of capital needed to build new plants, to upgrade equipment, to undertake research and product development, and to retrain workers.

These agreements would set precise directions and year-by-year targets. A change in course or a willful disregard of goals would trigger a cutoff in federal financial backing, a suspension that would last until progress resumed or another understanding came into force.

It will not be easy to develop or ratify these agreements. Precisely because of the importance and the difficulty of building these new partnerships, the President should assume visible responsibility for launching them. He should designate high-level officials from the Treasury, Labor, and Commerce departments to work with union, management, and investor representatives to identify the issues each agreement must address and to help in drafting responses that satisfy the fundamental interests of all parties.

Moreover, if negotiations stalemate, he should step in to moderate the give-and-take. This function is truly a presidential one. It is in such situations that the Chief Executive and no one else can define and assert the national interest, and move traditionally adversarial relationships, such as that between unions and management, off dead center and toward cooperation.

This process would start from the reality of government involvement in industrial development. It would reverse, however, the hit-or-miss pattern of the past by seeking to define and implement long-term objectives. And it should save not just effort, but money.

This process of reaching consensus would differ from past government involvement with individual industries in several important ways. First, government, industry, and labor would all be required to look ahead, to anticipate and address long-range problems and opportunities rather than reacting to emergencies with makeshift solutions.

Second, the process would not be *ad hoc,* nor merely a response to the "squeaky wheel." Unlike now, there would be no premium for being the first petitioner at the White House door.

And third, this process would emphasize give-and-take. Industrial assistance tied to modernization and growth agreements would do away with the unproductive giveaways and emergency aid that have become all too familiar. To the extent that tax abatements or credits, accelerated depreciation allowances, loans or guarantees, tariffs, quotas, and marketing agreements remained policy instruments, their use would be directly linked to agreements on making the industry more competitive.

The savings to the taxpayer should be large. By targeting, coordinating, and rationalizing direct and indirect government assistance to industry, present scattershot outlays could be reduced by one third to one half. Out of an annual total of over $300 billion, that would mean $100 billion–$150 billion saved. That is real money.

The goal of presidentially negotiated industrial-modernization agreements is to make basic American manufacturing industries the most modern and competitive in the world. The notion that we can rely on foreign autos, steel, chemicals, textiles, and other manufactured goods is unacceptable to me and to most Americans. We can and must compete, but it will not happen by protecting worn-out industries—or by accident.

Rewarding Risk

Our major industries, whether troubled or expanding, have a set of needs to which the most effective responses can be developed through a partnership for sustained growth. The most active, innovative, and diverse sector of the economy, however, is small business. It is here that much of our high-technology activity takes place—where companies like Apple and Atari emerge and become high fliers in a very short period of time.

Such companies, and new ones yet to be born, have needs that are vastly different from those of mature industries. The needs of small business can be principally defined by the single word: capital. They can be met by a series of reforms—mostly modest ones—to liberate existing financial institutions to reward initiative and encourage invention. We should put our money where we can use it—within the reach of American entrepreneurs.

They are the men and women who own and operate our 11 million small businesses. In the past they have been the major source of new jobs, new innovations, and, ultimately, much of our economic vitality. They are the developers of more than half the new products and services that have sprung up since World War II. They account for more than half the private sector's goods and services, employ nearly 60 percent of our work force, and provide, directly or indirectly, the livelihood of 100 million Americans.

With them, moreover, lies a vast potential for economic revitalization. One study of seventy-two companies backed by venture capitalists in the 1970s projected that by 1989, these firms would employ 500,000 to 2.5 million people and would be generating activity responsible for between $11 billion and $31 billion in yearly personal and corporate tax payments. Such results will spring from a total investment through 1979 of only $209 million.

We should be freely stocking this pool of energy and talent. Instead, too often, we seem to be starving it. Tight money makes start-up and expansion capital hard to obtain. Myriad government regulations stifle the entrepreneurial spirit. Sound ventures that should have good access to America's vast financial resources find, on the contrary, that it is difficult to begin and tough to grow. Usually they are crippled in competing for funds. Sometimes they are simply short of management skills and savvy. They need help in getting *both* forms of capital.

The major task of reform in this area is to open doors that are now either closed or too narrow. There are two related paths to pursue: easing regulations on private financial institutions and strengthening the activity of development centers in the states. This approach will engage both the public and the private sectors in a double-barreled blast against barriers to growth.

REGULATORY REFORMS Government-regulated financial institutions control most of the capital available to start new enterprises and to support existing ones as they diversify and modernize. Supply-side tax cuts—the centerpiece of Reaganomics—backed the wrong horse. By concentrating mainly on stimulating individual investors, they have ignored the $5 trillion asset pool held by financial institutions. Pension funds alone control 1,000 times as much as the $800 million invested as venture capital, primarily by individuals, in 1981. Commercial banks hold over $2 trillion in assets.

Conservative management of this money directs its huge investment potential away from risk-taking entrepreneurs. Regulations, moreover, discriminate against financing for small businesses. State "legal lists," for example, which govern investment by insurance companies and many public pension funds, set eligibility requirements so high that smaller firms cannot meet them. Recent financial deregulation measures have updated some of the means by which institutions may obtain their funds. Now we must also begin to remove or lessen the obstacles to *using* those funds productively to fuel the smaller-scale enterprises that are being shortchanged.

Derek Hansen, the former deputy superintendent of banking for the state of California, has proposed four such reforms that could yield substantial returns:

- Regulators could permit banks to identify loans that carry moderately higher risks than are normally accepted and to charge applicants for such funds slightly higher interest rates.
- A federal or state loan-loss reserve program could be established to insure a negotiated percentage of a commercial loan. It would be financed equally by the borrower, the lender, and the government.
- Commercial banks could be encouraged to make greater use of equity participation agreements by clarifying the rules that now cover such activities.
- The Community Reinvestment Act, which requires financial institutions to meet the credit needs of their communities with affirmative measures, could be broadened to stimulate productive business investment instead of focusing almost exclusively on housing and consumer loans.

These changes and others like them entail low costs and offer high returns. Were such reforms to divert just one tenth of 1 percent of the present asset base of regulated financial institutions to the needs of small business, investments in that sector would increase by $5 billion a year. Adding more to the entrepreneurial pool than the combined total of all Small Business Administration loans and all current venture-capital commitments, this shift would not compromise the soundness of the regulated financial sector. It could, however, bring substantial rewards for both the economy in general and institutional investors in particular.

STATE DEVELOPMENT AGENCIES As private-sector patterns change, public efforts to close the capital gap that hinders enterpreneurs must expand and be better targeted. Since 1970, more than thirty states have established new financial agencies for this purpose. Their structures and techniques vary. Some are controlled directly by the state; most are corporations under independent management. Some specialize in debt instruments; others, in the riskiest high-yield equity investments. Some follow a general mandate to sponsor growth in employment and diversification; others target high-technology industries or distressed communities. The best of them need to be encouraged. Their experiences point the way for others to follow.

One of the earliest state institutions was the Connecticut Product Development Corporation. It was founded in 1973 specifically to provide risk capital for ventures in new products. A state loan provided most of the initial funding, but the CPDC's innovative feature is its royalty agreement provision.

In return for a loan covering as much as 60 percent of a firm's costs in developing a product, the CPDC is entitled to a 5 percent royalty on the product's net sales, up to five times the amount of the loan. Such a deal puts no burden on the firm until sales bring in profits and does not intrude a state presence into the ownership of the business. The CPDC's loan-investments have already yielded it over $800,000 in royalty payments, a 15.3 percent return for the state's taxpayers. In 1981, CPDC-supported firms brought 300 new jobs and $11 million in product sales to Connecticut.

In a neighboring state, the Massachusetts Capital Resources

Company, begun in 1977 and capitalized by a $100 million investment fund from local insurance companies, focuses on high-risk projects whose activities promise a boost to employment and to the economy of their community. In return for participation in the fund, insurance firms earn considerable tax relief. Over four years, the MCRC has invested $71 million in sixty-three companies, with $49 million going to small enterprises. The infusion of capital has either created or maintained over 6,000 jobs in the state.

These success stories teach lessons for national application. While tailoring its own agencies to its specific needs, resources, and economy, each state should consider setting up not one but three such institutions: one for small-enterprise development in general, one for pioneering new technologies, and one for aid to depressed areas. Perhaps the federal government could act as an investor, putting capital into such institutions on a matching basis. Together, these channels for added capital could give America's entrepreneurs the financial boost they need in the form best suited to them.

TECHNICAL ASSISTANCE Among the most important lessons to be learned from the activities of existing state development programs is the need to match financial capital with managerial experience. Not every creator of a sound business idea has the practical skill to match his or her ingenuity, or the knowledge to take a project successfully through the difficult start-up phase and on to productive expansion. Too few have access to the educational and training backup available through programs such as the Small Business Development Center at the University of Georgia or the Small Business Institute of the State University of New York at Albany. States that seek to expand the financial capital available to entrepreneurs should also assist in getting their business schools involved with local firms, giving courses and sustaining research.

The Hawaii Entrepreneurship Training and Development

Institution (HETADI) has been showing the way since 1977 with a unique program that specializes in working with the socially deprived and with ethnic minorities. It reaches individuals eligible for Comprehensive Employment and Training Act (CETA) support and tuition-paying clients as well, giving basic and advanced training in business skills. It has done so well in identifying and preparing entrepreneurs that 55 percent of its graduates enjoyed business success equaled by only 10 percent of the business people in a control group.

Another government initiative of a different sort is the "one-stop" business development center. In Texas, the San Antonio Department of Economic and Employment Development not only provides financial aid through a wide variety of federal and state loan programs, but helps firms considering a move to the area to find the locations they want, obtain the permits they need, and get quick answers to questions about relevant regulations.

The energies and imagination of individual Americans offer us the strongest guarantee of our economic growth. Government at the federal, state, and local levels has to work to free their strengths, back their risk taking, elevate their skills, and set them firmly on the road that will bring rewards not just to them but to all of us.

Recycling Pension Funds

One of the potentially most powerful instruments of economic revitalization is also one of the least effectively used. Public and private pension funds, controlling over $800 billion in assets now, are already capable of making a massive contribution to industrial recovery. By 1995, the total is projected to reach an astounding $4 trillion. This could be a "made in America" answer to the Bank of Japan, which pours huge sums of money into leading Japanese industries.

The largest single source of investment capital, pension funds in 1982 bought an estimated 81 percent of all new stock issues and 44 percent of all new bond issues. If current trends hold, within a dozen years they will hold 65 to 75 percent of all publicly traded equities of American corporations. This enormous power, however, is sitting largely in Treasury securities, home mortgages, and conventional stocks and bonds that earn less overall than passbook savings accounts. And 94 percent of the stock holdings are concentrated in the nation's 500 largest companies, two thirds in the 100 biggest firms.

Investing in small firms or nontraditional ventures is discouraged for most pension funds. Most state laws require their investments be made conservatively. For example, California pension funds have been permitted to invest only in corporations worth over $100 million that had publicly traded stock and met rigid requirements on paying dividends.

Pension funds are creating a huge shift in the ownership of capital, a change unparalleled in dimension since the industrial middle class supplanted feudal property owners. But the millions of American workers who are taking indirect control of significant chunks of corporate America are not using the vast, collective influence they could wield to open new opportunities and creative alternatives to stimulate growth. The challenge is there, but those who could answer it best seem unaware of their potential.

Channeling just a small additional percentage of pension fund investments into newer, smaller ventures could contribute significantly to creating jobs and opportunities in the communities where the pensions are earned. Such investments could stimulate capital-starved industries such as housing, provide new farmers with start-up financing, and in general foster better-balanced regional economic development.

While social and financial returns would be high, risk could be kept low. Managers of pension fund portfolios, who cite their obligation to ensure their clients a secure retirement income to justify their concentration on the blue-chip stocks and bonds, should look more closely at the soundness of supposedly high-risk investment alternatives. They will find that the $450 million in 1979–1981 private-pension-fund "flings" in venture capital proved, in fact, to be both wise and safe. Two major recent studies of venture capital funds found they generate average returns of 20 and 45 percent. Significantly, no professionally managed venture capital fund has failed to earn positive overall returns.

To make imaginative investing the rule instead of the exception, we need four positive modifications in pension fund behavior (suggested by William Schweke of the Corporation for Enterprise Development). First, employees should take a larger role in deciding how their funds are invested. Second, lawmakers should revise the standards and goals for pension fund management. Third, states should expand the help and advice they provide pension fund managers. And finally, the managers should themselves become activists in developing new investment opportunities.

INCREASING EMPLOYEE PARTICIPATION Workers contributing to their own pension fund should have the right to representation on the board of trustees, and the opportunity to have a say in investment decisions that will affect the revitalization of their community. States and cities should set an example for private plans by requiring that employees be represented on the investment committees or boards that oversee state and local pension fund management.

RELAXING LEGAL RESTRICTIONS Public funds are now burdened by excessive and rigid constraints on the kinds of investments they can make. Private plans, by contrast, have the right under the Employee Retirement Income Security Act (ERISA) to weigh the merits of a specific venture on the basis of its value within the fund's total portfolio. New laws should give the public funds similar standards of what is prudent and emphasize, as well, a preference for in-state or local investments, the purchase of shares in small businesses, limited partnerships in venture capital firms, and real estate and mortgage instruments.

DEVELOPING INVESTMENT CLEARINGHOUSES States should help steer pension funds looking for innovative investment alternatives to opportunities they might not locate on their own. California's Pension Investment Unit, established in 1981, fills such a role for both public and private plan managers, helping them match their $60 billion in assets with projects for small-business expansion, new technology development, and affordable housing construction that meet the state's goals and the investors' interests. While few states can hope to generate as much capital as California—an estimated $930 million from pension funds in 1983—all can profit by establishing clearinghouses suited to their own resources and requirements. Such agencies would be able to collect and disseminate information on new investment options, recommend policies, design demonstration projects, develop new mechanisms for investment, and make it possible for pension fund managers to confer regularly and coordinate their strategies.

CREATING NEW OPPORTUNITIES Small business, housing, agriculture, and energy are high-priority fields for new investment. To develop them, however, states must take a more active role in marrying pension fund assets to specific projects. All these activities need the sort of reliable, "patient" money that pension plans can provide more readily than commercial banks and can continue to deliver as a new venture moves along the long road to profitability and expansion.

Although private pension funds have taken an active role in such developments, most public ones have been slow to follow. Two exceptions—both successful—can be found in Ohio and Washington. In Ohio, with authority to place up to 5 percent of its assets in nontraditional investments, the State Teachers Retirement System has backed seven venture-capital limited partnerships. The Washington State Investment Board has committed $26 million to five such projects. Following suit, other states should have their public pension fund managers earmark a small percentage of their assets for limited-partnership ventures, as well as for small-business investment corporations and minority enterprise small-business investment corporations, which are licensed by the Small Business Administration to provide equity capital and long-term debt to small businesses.

In the area of housing, Hawaii has more than a decade of experience in using public pension funds to provide below-market mortgages to home-buying public employees, a valuable stimulus to housing construction. California is starting a program for state workers that eliminates closing costs, permits lower down payments, and offers fixed-rate financing. Texas, Massachusetts, and New York pension funds are being used to buy packages of mortgages put together by private companies, and a Minnesota consortium of local retirement plans is sharing in home purchases made by middle-income families that need a partner to carry part of their down payment. What these states have explored, others can emulate in order to help public employees acquire housing they can afford and builders find the buyers they need.

In farming states, pension funds can help meet the desperate need of family farms for capital by buying the guaranteed portions of loan packages from the state agricultural finance institutions that grant them. Similarly, following the example of California's Business and Industrial Development Corporation, public funds can stimulate growth in energy conservation and efficiency by buying loans granted for renewable-energy-resource development. Such purchases from lending agencies not only recycle the initial loan capital, but allow the lender to multiply its capital base.

The possibilities for creative use of pension fund assets are almost limitless. The $3.2 trillion expansion of those assets over the next twelve years gives us enormous new resources to put into economic revitalization. We need only liberalize some of the rules that now restrict the application of pension plan dollars, and

develop the new ideas that will assure the country and fund bene-
ficiaries the highest, steadiest, most constructive return.

Maintaining Our Lead
in Research and Development

The sheer size of pension fund holdings, as well as insurance
reserves and bank holdings, ensures us the capital to finance a
decade of innovation. Another vital form of our national wealth is
scientific—the knowledge and ingenuity we need to create new
technologies and to maintain the pace of invention. Redirecting
pension plan investments is and should remain a private, local,
and state responsibility. Nurturing the resource base for technical
advance is, on the other hand, an important field for federal
action.

The need for action is great. Traditionally, the United States
has devoted a larger portion of its wealth to research and development and to scientific and technical training than other nations.
The benefits we have earned from such investments have been
crucial to our economic and military security. But in the 1970s,
our spending for these purposes dropped off from its previous
pace just as many of our foreign competitors were increasing
their activity and expenditures. American spending on R & D
declined as a percentage of GNP by more than 20 percent over
the past decade. Federal support reached a high in 1974 and has
slid steadily lower since.

Although we need to increase the level of government investment, we should be combining added federal funds with new
incentives for private research-and-development activity. Direct
federal assistance, for example, should be targeted on closing the
learning gap, specifically through National Science Foundation
grants that will enable universities to expand facilities and enroll-
ments in science and engineering courses, and to support faculty
and graduate student research.

At an absolutely basic level, we must reinvigorate the earliest government inducement to research and development—our patent laws. They must be strengthened to ensure protection for the products of R & D investments.

As the world's largest purchaser of high technology, especially through the Department of Defense, the federal government is already a leading contributor to innovation. The purchases it makes and the contracts it assigns need to be examined in a fresh light to see how these public funds can be directed to stimulate greater private-sector ingenuity and spin-offs of new products. Simply introducing a bias toward the acquisition of goods and services that spur technological progress could make a significant impact. If, for example, vehicle procurement policies at all levels of government rewarded improved safety, fuel economy, and pollution control, manufacturers competing for such a large market would have an added incentive to seek technical breakthroughs in those areas.

The most important help the federal government can provide, however, is in easing the access of private firms to the large supplies of capital needed for R & D programs. Such investment is expensive, and the expense may continue for a long time before income from innovation begins to make up for the initial outlays. With costs so high, it is not surprising that only twenty companies account for more than half of all American research and development activity. What *is* surprising—and possible to remedy—is the government policy that allocates only 3.5 percent of the federal R & D budget to small business. Expanding that share could bring large returns.

More broadly, the government should revise laws now in force that effectively narrow opportunities for R & D risk sharing, the most promising option for many firms that cannot afford large research and development efforts unless they can undertake them in cooperation with other companies. I have introduced legislation that would pave the way for such joint ventures by protecting companies meeting certain standards from antitrust action. What our laws now discourage we should be promoting.

To keep American technology in competition abroad, we must have our enterprises working together on the breakthrough scientific concepts they cannot afford to ignore or to develop separately.

Trade Policy for a Competitive America

America is engaged in a global economic contest of great risk but high promise. The arena is trade. In it, our major commercial rivals are also our most important political allies. From it can come either prosperity for all participants or failure and global depression. America's choice of policies will be crucial to the outcome.

Over two centuries ago, Tom Paine could exult that America was remote "from all the wrangling world." In place of that isolation, we are now inextricably engaged in the international economy. We are the strongest competitor, but that position is being fiercely challenged. We can no longer produce all that we need nor absorb at home all that we produce. We must have other markets and other suppliers, and we must have a strategy to ensure a growing global marketplace and an expanding American portion of the commerce in it.

We face this trade imperative at a time when the trends are most alarming and least favorable:

- In 1982, the volume of global trade fell, breaking the chain of steady increases since the early 1960s.
- In 1982, America's merchandise trade deficit set an all-time record, topping the 1978 peak figure of $34 billion.
- In 1980, America's share of the global market was declining for 71 percent of 102 manufactured commodities, while Germany's share was dropping for only 24 percent and Japan's for 26 percent.
- Even as we doubled our exports' share of the GNP from 4 to 8 percent between 1970 and 1982, we saw the United

States' share of world exports slide from 15 to 12 percent.
- We have a large and growing trade deficit with Japan, estimated at close to $20 billion for 1982.

We must recognize the reasons for these trade problems. Certainly, the one most often cited today—unfair trade practices of other nations—has played an important role. But it must be placed in proper perspective if we are to shape the right policy responses. For example, if the Japanese had removed every one of their trade barriers, this would have reduced our $16 billion deficit with them in 1981 by only $1 billion to $2 billion. As critical as they are, we must look beyond unfair trade practices.

Another fundamental reason for our weak merchandise trade position is the enormous increase in our oil import bills. Between 1973 and 1981, our payments for oil from abroad jumped from $8 billion to $78 billion. Had we bought no imported oil, we would have registered substantial merchandise trade surpluses in each of the last five years, reaching approximately $50 billion in 1981.

A less visible, but even more important, factor is the degree to which our exports are no longer competitively priced. In the period 1979–1981, for instance, the price of our goods to a foreigner paying dollars rose sharply compared to the price of similar goods from Japan and West Germany. This meant American products cost as much as 50 percent more than products of those two exporters and 25 percent more than those of all trading nations on average. A strong, overvalued dollar and higher inflation rates in the United States were the major reasons. The stronger the dollar—the more francs, marks, yen, pesos, or lire needed to buy a dollar—the more expensive our exports become and the fewer sales we make in markets where competitors can undersell us. Every percentage point of loss in competitive pricing is likely to produce an increase of $2 billion to $3 billion in our trade deficit.

In response to the stagnant state of both the world economy

in general and trade in particular, the most tempting solution is a return to the harsh protectionist measures we and other nations adopted during the global economic collapse half a century ago. But this would be the worst mistake we could make. Those policies were designed to strengthen domestic markets by keeping imports out, but their result was to shrink trade everywhere. Behind high tariff barriers, production dwindled and unemployment soared. The Great Depression became worldwide, and the political upheaval that accompanied it set the stage for World War II.

As pressures mount for similar protectionist policies in the 1980s, we cannot afford to forget the lesson of the 1930s. Today, we stand at a similar crossroads. One path leads toward unilateral policies to protect ourselves at the expense of our trading partners. The other course requires us to insist increasingly on an open world economy governed by multilateral treaties and agreements, particularly the thirty-five-year-old General Agreement on Tariffs and Trade (GATT). The latter is more difficult, but it is the only path that will produce real economic benefits for us and our allies.

Within the multilateral framework we can strengthen our own competitive position and fuel a trade expansion from which all nations can benefit. Without a framework for international commerce, trade wars would devastate the existing, precarious economic order, with incalculable political consequences. America has the power, through its choice of policies, to affect the choices others make. Our decision is critical for our own prosperity and that of the world.

PRINCIPLES AND PRAGMATISM The central premise for our actions must be the realization that, in trade, more is better. Our goal—except in imports of energy—is to keep our own markets as open as possible, so that nations selling to us will have the earnings to buy what we export. As the largest trader in the world, we gain when the purchasing power of other countries increases, when our goods and services can be brought at competitive prices on acceptable credit terms, and when foreign markets are as open as our own.

That situation is the ideal. We are now far from it. And unfortunately, our present problems are causing a divisive and misleading debate over whether our policy should be focused on free trade or on protectionism. Neither extreme is the right answer in view of today's economic realities. We cannot devise the best trade policy by blaming others for our problems. Nor can we ignore the difficulties our industries are facing as a result of growing—often unfair—trade competition.

The best trade strategy is based upon taking the offensive to make American industries more competitive. We need more balanced approaches to public investment priorities and money and credit supplies in order to reduce today's high interest rates—rates that not only stifle productive investment at home, but make the dollar (and our dollar-valued exports) overpriced abroad. We also need an industrial strategy to revitalize our basic industries and to promote the continued growth of high-technology and service industries.

All these efforts will be frustrated, however, if our trading partners adopt—as some of them already have—protectionist practices that restrict our access to their markets and disguise the real cost of their products within a maze of subsidies. For too long, America as the largest trader could ignore violations of international treaties and agreements. That is no longer the case.

When others break the rules, we must be quick and persistent in calling them to account. We must bring our complaints against unfair trade practices to GATT and press them vigorously. We have the right to insist that our partners and competitors fulfill their GATT obligations and stop objectionable practices. If the practices are not stopped, then we should exercise our right to seek compensation. The President has full authority to employ a wide range of measures to exercise our rights under GATT, including our right to retaliate if necessary. But only if all other steps fail should we consider retaliatory measures.

And in almost every case, temporary administrative sanctions are vastly preferable to statutory, legislated protectionism.

Retaliation is a prerogative to be exercised with great caution, for global interdependence means that any form of protection we erect for one of our industries will almost certainly be matched by our competitors' building obstacles against other products of ours. When we restrict access for European or Brazilian steel exporters, for instance, we give their governments grounds for shutting out our farm produce or earth-moving equipment. Individual trade measures do not occur in a vacuum. Before instituting sanctions, we must weigh the inevitable retaliatory effects.

We must also always bear in mind that such ripple effects may seriously erode our areas of real trading strength. In focusing on our many trade problems, we often tend to forget our areas of significant strength that must be promoted, not threatened:

- Services, such as banking and insurance, and investment income from overseas operations have contributed a net annual surplus of $30 billion to $40 billion in recent years.
- High-technology has also yielded annual trade surpluses of over $30 billion in the last few years.
- Agricultural exports, which rose by 500 percent in the past decade, made a $26 billion positive contribution to our trade balance in 1981.

The final result of the strong contributions by these sectors has been a dramatic reversal—the turning around of a 1978 current account (merchandise trade plus services) deficit of nearly $15 billion to a $4.5 billion surplus in 1981.

If, after taking the full range of both domestic and foreign implications into account, we still believe some form of interim relief is required, then we should follow a very specific path. The period of relief provided a battered domestic producer should be temporary, and it should be directly tied to specific actions on that industry's part to regain a competitive stance. The point of protecting an industry in trouble is to help it bounce back, and the pragmatic judgment we must make in such cases has to be based on an evaluation of that industry's importance to our economic security and its real prospects to succeed in global competition.

TRADE POLICY GOALS Our trade policy should have three major thrusts: achieving our full export potential, managing import problems and vigorously enforcing American trade rights, and strengthening and expanding the international trading system. We need such a three-pronged strategy because the trade challenges facing American industries are varied. Each sector of the economy faces a different set of problems requiring a different set of solutions.

There are basically four broad groups into which American industries can be divided. The first consists of industries that are, by and large, no longer competitive because their primary competition comes from developing countries with low wage scales—for example, certain parts of the metalworking and electronic components industries. The second group consists of industries that are not now competitive but could be, and whose competition comes primarily from developed countries—examples include both mature industries, such as steel and automobiles, and high-growth areas, such as video cassette recorders. A third category includes industries in which United States firms are very competitive, such as small computers and most kinds of machinery. For this category of exports, world markets are still relatively free from restrictions. The final category consists of industries that are competitive, but face international markets partially closed by procurement practices, tariffs, and nontariff barriers. Leading examples are agricultural products and telecommunications equipment.

No single trade solution can meet the needs of all four categories. Some industries would benefit most from export promotion, while others require temporary import relief measures and adjustment assistance, and still others need broader resolution of their difficulties through a strengthened and expanded GATT.

PROMOTING AMERICAN EXPORTS We are currently operating far below our export potential. Over 20,000 American companies that could be competing in international markets are not. If these 20,000 were trading, they could help reduce our chronic merchandise trade deficit while generating many new jobs and revenues.

One first step toward bringing more American players into action and giving them a better competitive stance was the passage in 1982 of the Export Trading Company Act. Liberalizing the application of banking, antitrust, and other regulations affecting exporters, this legislation should encourage small and medium-sized American firms to widen their foreign activities, pooling resources as their competitors often do to offer customers a broad range of financial, marketing, and distribution services along with competitively priced products. The new law is a sound measure. But it is also only a first step.

To realize our full potential, we must give international economic issues—and trade in particular—a much more central role in our economic policy making. This must be at the highest level of government. West European and Japanese leaders do not consider it trivial or demeaning to be aware of the major export orders their nation's businesses are seeking. But when did we last hear an American President speak authoritatively on exports?

More fundamentally, we must consider whether the current structure of government agencies promotes or inhibits positive action on trade. We should examine a variety of potential institutional reforms, ranging from requiring a member of the Council of Economic Advisers to be an international economics expert to establishing a Department of Trade and Industry that would bring together most trade-related activities in the federal government.

Next, we must address the important issue of export financing support. Foreign buyers of "big ticket" capital goods increasingly select their suppliers based upon the most advantageous financing offered. Many foreign exporters may offer purchasers more financial aid from their governments than our Export-Import Bank is authorized to do. As a result, our companies are basically in a defensive trading position.

The ideal objective should be the elimination of all government subsidies. Until that time, our system should make it possible for a foreign purchaser to buy American products by borrowing in America. When commercial credit costs too much—compared to what other nations are willing to offer—United States companies should be able to count on the resources of the Export-Import Bank to assist them in concluding a sale. The Reagan Administration has sought to reduce investment in Ex-Im Bank operations. We should ensure that the bank, instead, has adequate assets to deploy. This would not only promote increased exports, but would also translate into more jobs for Americans—2,400 jobs for every $100 million of Ex-Im Bank–financed exports.

Such an allocation of resources would demonstrate a new determination to give priority to export promotion. That commitment is essential. It has to emanate from the highest levels of the federal government—from a President who does not hesitate to connect diplomacy with trade expansion—in order to give American businesses both tangible and psychological backing for an export campaign.

We must also directly attack the knowledge barrier hindering export expansion. Americans, who long ago mastered the art of salesmanship at home, have not put their expertise into practice abroad, either because we lacked awareness of the opportunities or because unfamiliarity with other cultures and confidence in our own made us hesitant to take on overseas challenges.

Fortunately, a mechanism exists to help: the Foreign Commercial Service. This service has been significantly strengthened in the past few years, placing knowledgeable individuals in sixty-seven countries to advise on American export opportunities. We should continue to expand this service until the appropriate number of people are in place throughout our embassies in order to take full advantage of export markets. We need commercial attachés in every major embassy identifying profitable opportunities abroad, developing connections to foreign marketing and distribution networks, and guiding potential exporters through the maze of foreign rules, regulations, and cultural barriers.

Especially in third-world countries—the most competitive and (except for their heavy debt loads) promising markets—American businesses need the information and guidance that officers in the Foreign Commercial Service can provide. Dealing more with government purchasers than with private entrepreneurs like themselves, American exporters require the diplomatic sensitivity and acumen, the knowledge of the territory and prospects, and the access to foreign officials that our trade officials can more easily provide.

City and state governments can also assist in breaking down the knowledge barrier by making export information services and facilities available, accessible, and appropriate for local businesses. In stimulating them to become more export oriented and by actually facilitating exports, local communities can also foster their own economic growth and development.

Finally, the United States must recognize that much of the potential for significant growth in our exports lies in the markets of developing nations. Latin America is a case in point. For years, Japan has been busy building current and future markets in Latin America for its high-technology wares. It has built manufacturing facilities in the importer nations, licensed Latin Americans to produce components of Japanese design, and even constructed entire plants for local ownership. Instead of putting intensive but short-lived effort into bidding for one contract at a time, Japan has established a continuous presence and a continuing commercial relationship with private and governmental customers. Such a policy requires a willingness to invest time and money now for reliable, long-term returns rather than high, immediate profits.

This may not be the exact model we want for United States companies, particularly while United States unemployment is high, but American firms must also look beyond their one-year balance sheets and invest for the years and decades of expansion to come. After three decades of the Japanese learning from us about new technologies, it is time we learned how to vigorously establish export beachheads to build on in the years ahead.

Beyond these general export-oriented actions, there are specific needs that must be addressed, particularly for two of our historically strong export sectors—agriculture and high technology—that are currently facing serious difficulties and challenges.

For some time, America has been referred to as the breadbasket of the world—and for good reason. One of every three acres of United States farmland is planted for export; the total value of American agricultural exports in 1981 alone was $43 billion. But for the first time in a decade, our commodity exports dropped at least 10 percent in value in 1982. Moreover, mountains of surplus grain are now building up in the nation's storage bins, equaling nearly a year's domestic consumption.

These are very serious developments, for agriculture relies significantly more on exports than does American industry in general. But added to the decline in demand and rise in supply are chronic and severe protectionist practices by other producing nations. Every market economy, including ours, has extensive government intervention in agriculture—price supports, purchase programs, and so forth. But the European Community goes further by subsidizing exports of agricultural production. This practice must be addressed. Yet the GATT has failed to act on the numerous complaints filed by the United States and to force the Europeans to curtail their use of illegal subsidies.

We can no longer sit by while farmers go out of business and young people have no chance of getting into farming. The United States must protect its rights by making the rules of the GATT work. Until the Europeans substantially reduce their subsidies, the United States can begin a carefully targeted subsidies program limited to particular products and markets. There are substantial funds in the Commodity Credit Corporation that can be used to promote exports by subsidized financing.

The fundamental goal is to bring prices into line with market conditions. How each country achieves this goal should be its own decision, but serious GATT negotiations on domestic farm supports should also be considered. Instead of each government maintaining high price supports, we should encourage more programs like our own to withdraw some farmland from production, at least until better international distribution systems come into play and economic recovery widens demand.

Finally, as the most efficient and successful farmers in the world, Americans have an overriding interest in the expansion of agricultural trade. We also have a duty to ourselves to be reliable suppliers. Our 1973 embargo on soybeans hurt our standing badly, especially with Japan. The 1980 restrictions on grain sales to the Soviet Union raised further question about our steadiness of purpose and policy. American food exports should not be used as a political or diplomatic weapon. This practice both erodes America's reputation as a reliable food supplier and causes unnecessary and irreparable harm to our farmers. We must rebuild our reputation for dependability in order to maintain our position in international markets, at the same time as we use GATT to its fullest potential to make competition in those markets orderly.

In the high-technology area, as with agriculture, the United States' leadership position is being attacked and eroded on many fronts. But the most significant challenge by far comes from Japan, a nation that in the early 1970s made a national commitment to rapid and widespread development and diffusion of high-technology products. They have made tremendous progress, exemplified by their capturing 70 percent of the American market for 64K memory chips, the key state-of-the-art components of many products throughout our economy. Meanwhile, due to a variety of nontariff barriers, American companies have had great difficulty in gaining access to the large and lucrative

Japanese market for high-technology products. To attack this market access problem, I introduced in 1982, with Senators John Heinz and Alan Cranston, the High Technology Trade Act. The bill's main provision asserts a United States commitment to foreign treatment for our high-technology products equal to that given to local products. It also establishes a system to monitor, and remedy through negotiations, practices abroad that may adversely affect American high-technology trade and investment.

The bill is an important step, but it is only a first step. To fully meet the Japanese high-technology challenge, the United States must engage in a broad-scale high-technology offensive of its own, so it may remain competitive in this critical high-growth sector.

MANAGING IMPORTS We must meet these export challenges at the same time as we strengthen the performance and prospects of domestic industries fighting heavy foreign competition. The first step is to develop an overall industrial strategy to get through a period of sluggish global demand, preserve our vital, basic industrial capacity, and help new high-growth businesses. No amount of protectionism at our borders can match the benefits of making our domestic industries more competitive.

In this period of global recession and new sources of competition, however, some trade problems will intensify and some industries will suffer injury. The GATT system has a set of procedures, outlined above, under which nations can seek a halt to unfair trade practices and compensation for injury by another country's objectionable trade practices.

Unfortunately, while successive Administrations have supported the principles of GATT, they have not always vigorously and adequately protected American rights. We must convince our competitors that we will take strong action consistent with GATT and domestic law to ensure that our rights and international obligations are fulfilled and protected.

Because such procedures will not shelter all American workers from the effect of foreign imports, the United States must have an effective trade adjustment program. The original premise on which the Trade Adjustment Assistance program was based twenty years ago is just as valid today: we need a trade-specific adjustment program to cope with the problems of trade-affected Americans and to allow the United States to continue reaping the benefits of an open trading system.

The trade adjustment program must be revitalized. Its focus should be on retraining and employment subsidies rather than simple income transfers. The program could be at least partially funded by earmarking import tariff revenues for adjustment purposes.

STRENGTHENING AND EXPANDING GATT The final item on the agenda must be a strengthening and expansion of the multilateral trading system, GATT. This eighty-eight-nation institution holds the key to a stable world economic order. But in recent years many long-standing disputes have been left unresolved. Each of these areas—agriculture, steel, textiles and apparel, safeguards, and subsidies—constitutes a very significant element of world trade. In November 1982, at the GATT ministerial conference in Geneva, much time was taken up by the agricultural issue—with little accomplished on other issues. We need a new round of better-prepared, serious negotiations to address those issues, strengthen GATT, and relieve tensions among world trading partners.

In addition, we should expand GATT coverage to include trade in services, foreign investment, and high technology, as well as trade in goods. This is of vital importance to the United States because services and high technology are our leading export performers. Nontariff barriers, such as performance standards and restrictive government procurement and licensing practices, in these areas are especially troublesome and should be considered under GATT.

THE TRADE IMPERATIVE We must, in conclusion, transform the way we trade and the way we think about trading. Our current policy is largely defined by defensive measures such as embargoes, dumping complaints, antitrust challenges, and quotas. The pressure to build new protectionist barriers is fierce.

The correct policy, however, is an expansionist one. It puts our priority on trade liberalization and it connects an industrial revitalization strategy at home with efforts to make our producers more competitive and more extensively engaged abroad.

We must also use trade to draw our friends more closely to us, recognizing that a sound trade policy is as important to our national security as a strong defense. One without the other is a false security.

A thriving international economy in which countries are bound to one another as buyers and sellers, suppliers and markets, is far less prone to conflict than a stagnant, each-nation-for-itself world. In rallying the West and the developing nations for prolonged competition with Communist nations, we Americans can bring our enormous economic strengths to bear on building a buoyant world economy through trade expansion. In that setting, with the fruits of prosperity widely shared, we will find the best guarantee of our own security.

Instilling Vision and Foresight

Taken together, the elements of a new and comprehensive industrial policy outlined in the preceding pages make for an ambitious undertaking. Yet the prescription would be incomplete without addressing a fundamental failing of our government and corporate structures—shortsightedness. The speed with which technological and political changes can affect economic security—witness the 1973 oil crisis—makes our historically haphazard approach to identifying emerging issues a dangerous relic of a bygone era of leisurely economic evolution.

To expand the vision of government and private enterprise, a number of institutional obstacles must be overcome.

Business myopia is rooted in the often conflicting demands of short-term profits and more speculative long-term security and stability. Proper management and technological innovation in a fiercely competitive world market require attention to long-term returns, a willingness to accept risk, a dedication to quality control. In too many American firms, the conflict is being resolved in favor of short-term profits. If this keeps up, the result will be smaller long-term profits, lower quality, and eventual decline in market share.

Whatever can be said of industry's myopic vision can be said twice over regarding government. Congress appropriates funds on a specific, categorical, one-year-at-a-time basis, with little long-range perspective. In the executive branch, some agencies do develop long-range projections and forecasts, but often feel pressured to make them support current Administration policy and budget estimates—which means they get "adjusted." Government bodies face so many immediate problems that they find it difficult to develop effective long-range goals and strategies.

A basic reason for the absence of long-range vision is that "future accountability" is not built into the political system. The United States lacks any institutional framework within which to assess and address large-scale, long-term issues. In a fast-paced world economy, we need a new mechanism for anticipating and identifying trends.

We should establish a Council on Emerging Issues that would serve as an early warning system on changes and challenges before they surface as crises in the political arena. The national reaction to this kind of idea is usually "Oh no, not another government body." I share such general skepticism about creating new government agencies.

An exception is required in this instance because a federal government with over 2 million civilian employees does not have one group taking a serious, ongoing look at the future. This need not be a new bureaucracy. A council committed to long-range forecasting need have a permanent staff no larger than thirty to fifty people, like the Council of Economic Advisers (CEA). Such a body would serve as a complement to the CEA, which most often has a two-week time horizon.

The new council could perform the following functions: monitoring major long-run economic trends and analyzing their implications; reporting to the President on the prospects and needs of American industry; providing information for the development and negotiation of industrial modernization and growth agreements; forecasting international demographic, agricultural, natural resource, and industrial trends. In short, such expert analysis could provide the factual base upon which our political leadership would build our economic future. Properly directed, this undertaking would provide an enormous return on our investment.

Importantly, the council would have full access to information and projections, but no authority to implement policy. It should have no formal power other than that of persuasion and the prestige that comes from an important presidential advisory role. It would not be a planning body in the sense of establishing objectives for the future or picking winners and losers among our industries. Rather, it would anticipate and identify trends so the actual response to them could be conducted at the appropriate industrial or governmental level.

We must know in a more systematic fashion where we are so that we can decide more intelligently where we are going. We must investigate our future so that its challenges become our opportunities, not our downfall.

Granted, providing such early warning may be more of an art form than a science. Nevertheless, we now face fast-breaking economic changes of enormous magnitude and are without any organized means of anticipating their consequences. As Lord Keynes gently suggested, "There will be no harm in making mild preparations for our destiny."

An industrial strategy for America can help to make our industries efficient, productive, and internationally competitive. It springs from the recognition that we must supplement sound monetary and fiscal policies with a set of innovative, flexible policies and incentives that will seize the challenges faced by our industries and turn them into opportunities.

An industrial policy cannot, by itself, cure inflation, restore healthy rates of productivity, or remedy trade imbalances. But it could help put these problems into better focus and provide more effective measures for attacking them.

This is not a job for government alone. It requires agreement among all three principal economic actors—business, labor, and government. Such agreement is no longer a luxury. We simply must move forward together in this era of unprecedented foreign economic competition.

We must harness this nation's vast physical, financial, technical, and human resources to a new national resolve to make American industry globally competitive. This national resolve would be the 1980s equivalent of our 1960s commitment to space exploration.

A NEW
EMPLOYMENT
STRATEGY

———◆———

The skill, dexterity and knowledge
of a nation's people is the most powerful
engine of its economic growth.

—ADAM SMITH
The Wealth of Nations

Adam Smith's 200-year-old assessment is more valid today than ever before. Yet we are wasting the minds and muscle of over 20 million Americans who are either unemployed, working part-time involuntarily, or have given up looking for work. The human suffering of these jobless and underemployed men and women is a moral tragedy. But the sacrifice of their skills and energies represents a second kind of loss to our nation's strength, the needless depletion of our strongest and most important asset—people.

Human capital is the most productive, flexible, and responsive element of growth. We cannot afford to continue letting this vital resource either lie idle or decline in value. We need urgent measures to create productive employment and overcome the effects of the current recession. Fundamentally we also need a new employment strategy that invests in our human assets to obtain the highest and most productive return for the economy, the nation, and the workers themselves. That program—one that requires the combined, sustained efforts of labor, business, and government on all levels—is the subject of this chapter.

Challenges Today and Tomorrow

We are used to thinking of investment in terms of physical plant and equipment. We must recognize that the health, education, and trained skills of our citizens are even more valuable. The industries of the future will depend less for their success on physical hardware than on the human ingenuity that will hone America's technological edge. Investment today in people—in training our youth and retraining experienced workers—will earn huge dividends in the near future. And what we neglect today in basic and advanced education will soon return to haunt and eventually cripple us.

Our employment strategy for the 1980s must focus on three challenges.

First, we need more jobs—not just to turn recession into recovery, but to ensure opportunity for new entrants into the labor market and for those who are certain to be displaced by technological change and the shift from traditional manufacturing to new fields of enterprise.

We need more skilled workers now and will need far more workers with new skills in the near future—to increase productivity and to preserve for the United States the momentum that keeps ours a revolutionary society in a revolutionary time. We know technology will displace millions of workers in existing manufacturing jobs. And while new technology will create many new employment opportunities, we are beginning to see a widening gap between the jobs that need to be filled and the skills of job hunters. Without a major effort by a private and public partnership the mismatch will only get worse.

And we need more imagination and experimentation in the

workplace itself, to expand the scope for the individual as dramatically as machines are expanding the range of tasks workers perform. We must find ways to make such employment—whether in services, manufacturing, or agriculture—satisfying, creative, and fulfilling, for all Americans increasingly seek more than a paycheck. We all want challenge, a feeling of accomplishment, and a sense that our own contribution and individual talents are being used to the maximum.

JOB SEEKERS One way to measure the dimensions of the challenge is in raw numbers. There were 105 million Americans in the labor force in 1980. There will be between 122 million and 128 million in 1990. We have less than ten years in which to create 20 million jobs, twice as many as we brought into being between 1973 and 1980. We must grow at a rate even faster than we did during the boom years after World War II.

And we must make this effort at a time when deindustrialization is closing old plants and familiar doors. In the 1970s, by one estimate, such shutdowns cost us between 32 million and 38 million jobs. The pace has not slackened and the impact is nationwide. In the Frostbelt, in the past decade, for every 100 new jobs, 118 disappeared. And while the Northeast from Maine to Pennsylvania experienced the largest absolute number of shutdowns of large manufacturing plants, the South was far from immune. There the percentage of large manufacturing establishments open in 1970 and closed by 1979 was higher than anywhere else. In California, moreover, 100,000 workers were displaced by shutdowns in 1980 and 1981.

THE JOB MARKET MISMATCH These figures speak only to the size—not the shape—of the task we face. The picture becomes clearer, both more daunting and more challenging, if we try to determine the fields that will generate new demand for labor. While some will be low on the ladder of skills, most of the growing opportunities can be taken only by men and women able to handle sophisticated machinery and concepts. Fast-food chains may have places for 800,000 more employees by 1990, but millions of new jobs opening up by then will require special and specialized skills, some of them in wholly new lines of work. A major part of the challenge, then, will be to equip men and women to fill the jobs technological change is bringing into being.

According to some projections, new employment for almost 5 million Americans can be expected in fields where relatively few people work now. Consider these categories and estimated numbers of new jobs available in 1990:

Energy technician	650,000
Housing rehabilitation technician	500,000
Hazardous-waste management technician	300,000
Industrial laser process technician	600,000
Industrial robot production technician	800,000
Materials utilization technician	400,000
Genetic engineering technician	250,000
Bionic-electronic technician	200,000
Paramedic	400,000
Geriatric social worker	700,000

Many more new employment opportunities between 1978 and 1990 will consist of openings for data-processing machine mechanics, paralegal personnel, computer systems analysts, office machine and cash register service personnel, and computer programmers. Five of these six fields focus directly on the new information technologies. Only trained technical paraprofessionals can fill such jobs. But the supply of them is already short and is not expanding at anything like the required rate.

EDUCATION Instead of anticipating the challenge of preparing people for these new jobs, we are already falling behind. The Electronics Industry Association estimates, for instance, a need for nearly 200,000 engineers in 1985, but acknowledges that universities, given the teaching staff now in place, can only graduate 70,000 candidates. Add the demand for skills in such growth areas as genetics, lasers, energy, and robotics, and it is easy to see the widening gap between the intellectual tools we have and those we need.

Education is our first line of economic defense. But it has been systemically weakened by Reaganomic budget cutting. Inheriting a situation that called for increased investment, the Administration chose to neglect the needs of elementary and secondary schools across the country and to slash support for higher education. Just when the Information Revolution requires young Americans to increase their competence in science and mathematics and when economic interdependence obliges us to master other languages in order to compete effectively abroad, we are letting our technical schooling erode and our foreign language studies decline.

The statistics are frightening. Fewer than one American high school student in ten takes even one year of physics. American children study only one third to one half of the math and science drilled into their Japanese and Soviet contemporaries. Among nineteen countries where students were ranked according to their knowledge of science, Japan stood first and America fifteenth. Only 15 percent of our high schoolers take any foreign language course and only 4 high school graduates out of 100 study a foreign language for more than two years. In China, by contrast, the number of students and adults studying English exceeds the number of English speakers in the United States.

At the college and university level the situation is as bad or worse. While Japan graduates more engineers per year than we do, 10 percent of our undergraduate engineering faculty posts are either vacant or filled by temporary instructors. Between 1963 and 1980, as private industry recruited young scientists, the number of science and engineering teaching jobs held by new Ph.D.'s dropped by nearly 50 percent. Our best and brightest went into business. Their successors still in training, and needing highly technical instruction, pay a heavy price.

To add to the problem, more than a third of the doctoral degrees awarded by American universities in engineering in 1981 went to citizens of other nations here on temporary visas.

Ignoring these dangerous gaps in the vital scientific fields, the Reagan budget makers widened the damage to higher education in general. Proposing a 35 percent cut in federal aid to education overall and a 40 percent cut in some grants that would eliminate 1 million students, the President actually:

- cut the number of students receiving guaranteed loans from 3.5 million in 1981 to 2.9 million in 1982 and 2.1 million in 1983.
- eliminated the student benefits program under Social Security, aid that went to 640,000 children of deceased workers.
- blocked 230,000 students from getting work-study aid in 1983 and 300,000 more from receiving National Direct Student Loans.

Reductions in federal spending on higher education programs—Basic Educational Opportunity Grants, Supplemental Educational Opportunity Grants, and National Direct Student Loans—have been a serious blow to the opportunity of all young Americans to achieve an education. These programs helped move our country out of an era when higher education was open only to an economic elite.

Such programs should not be thoughtlessly tossed aside solely to reduce budget deficits. Public policy must foster the democratic principle that the academic doors of this nation should be open wide to all who can qualify, regardless of financial standing.

These senseless reductions represent a policy of active disinvestment in education.

TRAINING AND RETRAINING The Reagan policy of shortchanging the future also includes an assault on federal support for job training programs. While public service employment under CETA was phased out—escalating joblessness as recession worsened—the money saved was not transferred to training. Instead, federal support for such programs was reduced 23 percent in 1982, from $5.3 billion to $4.1 billion, with a further cut to $2.17 billion proposed for 1983.

It is essential to realize that most of the applicants for the positions to be created over the next twenty years are already in the work force. Over 90 percent of those who will be employed in 1990, and over 75 percent of those who will hold jobs in 2000, are adults now. Their skills are rapidly going out of date. They are the ones who must be retrained. And just to achieve that retraining for 1 or 2 percent of the work force each year—the rate West Europeans have managed to maintain—will require the United States to retrain 1 million to 2 million Americans annually. Much of that transformation will come through private initiative. But for it to succeed, we must have a clear and strongly supported national strategy for training and retraining.

At present we have anything but that. Between 1976 and 1980, for instance, we spent $16 billion on unemployment benefits, and only $53 million of the total was applied to helping workers train for and find new jobs. Tax policy compounds the misapplication of resources by rewarding investment in physical, but not human, resources. In 1981, American firms spent over $3,300 per worker on new plant and equipment and only $300 per worker on training. Finally, government efforts to assist the displaced are disorganized and ineffective. There is now a hodgepodge of twenty-two separate assistance programs, each of which operates independently of the others, none of which reaches more than a minuscule number of those in need.

ON-THE-JOB INNOVATIONS Workers today want more than a paycheck. The reward of a job well done, a job that gives free rein to creativity, that fosters a sense of real participation, is important to a new generation in the American work force. Changing social values and rising expectations, combined with economic strains on industry profits and job security, are putting greater pressures on employees and firms to find new ways to work cooperatively on the problems of productivity and job satisfaction.

Adam Smith's "economic man" was never the whole man for America's founders. They defined the pursuit of happiness—not of wealth or property—as a fundamental right. They saw that prosperity is not an end in itself but a means to bring genuine goals—quality and equality—closer to our grasp. In an epoch of upheaval those original principles remain basic. They must be applied to the way we work through what Theodore Roszak has called "a nobler economics that is not afraid to discuss spirit and conscience, moral purpose and the meaning of life."

In the pages that follow I outline a number of specific programs, some already tried and others still to be tested, to turn job seekers into job holders and to turn job holders into fulfilled workers. We must do nothing less than retool our talents, convert manpower to mind power.

Fortunately, we have both the resources to finance such an effort and the diverse agents—education, industry, labor, and government—to carry it out. The first requirement is to mobilize all of them to accomplish the same purpose. The second is to ensure that government action is targeted on sustaining the drive by using existing and new funding in concert with private initiative.

Teaching Tomorrow's Skills

"Human history," wrote H. G. Wells in 1920, "becomes more and more a race between education and catastrophe." The concept is one that Americans have long understood instinctively but acted on only spasmodically. In 1958, the year after the Soviet Union launched the first sputnik, the United States responded with a crash program to strengthen the teaching of mathematics, science, and foreign languages. Almost overnight we brought our education system into the twentieth century. The vehicle for the change was the National Defense Education Act. As Lyndon

Johnson, then Senate majority leader, told his colleagues just before the law was passed, "The billions of dollars that we have spent on missiles, planes, guns, ships, radar and other implements of modern war could easily become another Maginot Line. The instruments are worthless if we do not have educated minds to control them."

Twenty-five years later we need to renew the commitment to education made under the prodding of the Soviet coup in space. This time, however, the threat is not above our planet. It is, quite specifically, here and now in our failure to graduate young people able to master the basic instruments of progress in the Information Age.

We must dramatically improve our schools on two levels: the quality of basic instruction and the quantity of technical learning. Our aim must be to mold not just technologically competent graduates, but also citizens with the background in our history, our literature, and our values that can equip them to live fully and choose wisely in a time of technological revolution. José Ortega y Gasset, in his classic *The Revolt of the Masses,* warned that twentieth-century man could become a technologically competent barbarian without classical education. True education gives us understanding of our culture and our values, our history and literature and religion. Without it, we cannot hope for a society that does more than lurch blindly from crisis to crisis, unable to see where it has been and thus know where it should go.

Traditionally and properly, the initial responsibility for such education falls on parents and on the local and state governmental bodies they elect and can most effectively oversee. That pattern should not change, but the federal government should provide a sustained financial base to elevate the level of mathematical, scientific, and linguistic instruction in our elementary and secondary schools.

THE AMERICAN DEFENSE EDUCATION ACT In June 1982, I proposed legislation designed to answer this clear need. It would increase financial support for school districts that seek to improve the technical training they now provide. It would not override local energies, but would harness federal resources to help local institutions pull a heavier load.

The American Defense Education Act provides incentives and support to schools that, first, set targets for improving the instruction they offer in mathematics, the sciences, communications skills, foreign languages, and technology and, second, meet the goals they have established. School districts would be entitled to a basic payment of 2 percent of the average per-pupil expenditure in the state, but not less than the average per-pupil expenditure in the United States. Districts that achieve the targets they have set in the first year would get continued financial support equal to the initial incentive.

This proposal could be expensive—it would cost $4 billion a year if every one of the country's 16,000 school districts applied, qualified, and performed well. The cost of educational investment is high. The cost of ignorance is far higher.

HIGH-TECHNOLOGY MORRILL ACT The need for a new emphasis in our educational system is found not only at the elementary and secondary levels. We are not graduating enough scientists and engineers at the university level to meet the demands of the next two decades.

The solution will require many steps: special government-business fellowships for top-quality teaching faculty in critical fields, higher salaries to keep talented teachers from leaving their profession to obtain better-paying jobs elsewhere, and more up-to-date equipment at our universities. It certainly will require greater government support for education.

There is a model—over 100 years old—for what we need to do today. In 1862, more than a century ago, Congress passed the Morrill Land-Grant College Act. It eventually transferred more than 13 million acres of federal land to the states to stimulate the establishment of agricultural and industrial colleges, and brought sixty-nine institutiuons into being, including such schools as Cornell, the University of Illinois, and the Massachusetts Institute of Technology. It led to the establishment of agricultural extension programs and the growth of modern farming in the United States. Today, we lead the world in agricultural exports—not only because of rich and fertile land, but also because the Morrill Act brought government, education, and the agricultural community together in a national policy for growth.

This act is an excellent model for moving us into the era of high technology. Instead of land, however, the federal government should make available grants of money, to match the contributions of business and state governments to institutions of higher education that are establishing or expanding high-technology instruction.

This new partnership among federal, state, and local governments and private interests makes sense. Industry is best positioned to know its needs for skilled technicians and to know, as well, the gap between supply and demand. Universities, consulting with local firms on the courses to be taught, are best equipped to close the gap. Where schools and businesses take the first steps to set up or bolster such teaching, state and federal funding should be available to carry the process forward. Only firm financial commitments by business and state government would trigger the federal grants. Additionally, federal support would be limited to new programs or expansions of old ones that offered training in the most advanced technologies.

Most importantly, perhaps, such a high-technology successor to the Morrill Act would reestablish the principle, laid down by the original law, that education, when open to all and focused on practical needs, is a direct contributor to economic growth.

Building the Bridge from School to Jobs

Renewing our commitment to educational excellence and our support for training tomorrow's workers is an essential first step. But it will not, by itself, pave the way from school to job. Far too many high school and even college graduates today find that their diploma is only an admission ticket to the unemployment line. In the fall of 1982 teenage joblessness stood at 24 percent, and among minority youth the rate was nearly double—a staggering 47 percent. Our society cannot remain healthy by denying hope to those on whom its future depends.

Training for our young people must become more directly linked to job opportunities. This is especially critical as we move into a period when many existing types of job are disappearing and new ones are being rapidly created. Our youth must learn skills that can actually result in employment.

BASIC TRAINING The disadvantaged, especially minority youths and adults without basic or specific jobs skills, are unlikely to have access to training opportunities and are least able to pay for their own training. Developing fundamental and job-specific skills in this pool of potential entry-level workers would help ease unacceptably high levels of minority youth unemployment. Such programs would also help to fill an important gap in future labor markets, as demographic trends signal a coming shortage of new workers to fill entry-level jobs.

America must not waste these valuable human resources. Contrary to popular opinion, many federally supported youth and adult training programs have been effective both in developing basic skills and in moving previously hard-to-employ individuals into productive jobs.

CETA *training* programs (as distinct from the CETA public service jobs program), the Job Corps, and on-the-job and classroom training programs for adults (especially women) have all proved to be good investments for society. The Basic Educational Opportunity Grants program, providing small stipends to low-income individuals attending accredited colleges, has also stimulated greater educational achievement among the disadvantaged. Such successful programs should be expanded.

TRAINING FOR EMPLOYMENT We must also work to connect vocational training directly to the job market. If employers are not hiring welders or seamstresses but are looking for computer programmers and electricians, students should be learning the skills in demand, not necessarily the traditional entry-level capabilities.

To ensure there is a direct relationship between technical education and prospective employment, we should replace the Vocational Education Act of 1965—expiring in 1983—with a measure that patterns federal programs after the successful experiences of North and South Carolina, Georgia, and Oklahoma. In those states, schools and local firms combined efforts to design "customized" training courses that give students the skills to meet the needs of specific employers. Successful graduates of such programs in these four states not only get interviews with company personnel directors; usually they also get hired. Such programs still need some refinement and improvement to train students for mid-level jobs and jobs with real advancement possibilities. One program with this focus is the three-year-old California Worksite Education and Training Act.

While students with the right training will have an easier time entering the job market than others, many of them will need something extra: preparation for job hunting itself. This, too, is a skill that can be taught.

One state's initiative—Delaware's, in 1978—has shown a way to use the education system as a bridge to help students become workers. Faced with a 45 percent unemployment rate among sixteen- to twenty-four-year-olds, a small committee of state officials, educators, labor leaders, and private employers developed the yearlong counseling program for high school seniors called Jobs for Delaware Graduates. It taught students how to seek employment, how to dress for an interview, how to prepare a résumé, and what to expect at work. The program has successfully placed 86 percent of its participants in either full-time jobs or further schooling and, in 1981, put 935 seniors into jobs at a cost of about $1,400 per placement—less than one fourth of the cost of the least expensive CETA program.

Delaware's example has been followed in Tennessee, Arizona, Massachusetts, and Missouri, with the first three states reporting placement rates of 77 to 98 percent. Virginia and

Michigan are following suit, and a nonprofit corporation is now sponsoring spin-offs under the title Jobs for America's Graduates.

Another Delaware experiment that has become national in scope is 70001, Limited, the "Youth Employment Company." Focusing on the hardest-to-employ—school dropouts and juvenile offenders, as well as some disadvantaged adults—the Delaware program was launched by a grant in 1969 from the Thom McAn company, but became a private firm with U.S. Department of Labor funding in 1976. Since then it has placed over 11,000 participants in jobs in twenty-one states, giving them preemployment training emphasizing both motivation and skills. Paying no stipends, the program turns its graduates into wage earners at higher salary levels than those with similar handicaps, but no special preparation, can expect. One recent study showed that 70001 participants are able to pay back the program's costs out of their increased earnings in about a year.

Perhaps this program's most important innovation is the way in which it puts counseling, training, job placement help, and instruction all under one roof. Programs providing the same services separately cannot match the resulting economies of scale. And 70001 serves as a model for cooperative effort in integrating business, educational, and government resources to spur youth employment.

An entire generation is on the brink—poised either to take productive roles in society or to contribute to and compound the problems caused by the current shortcomings of our educational system. We have the experience, the means, and the power to make the right choice. We cannot escape the consequences of making the wrong one.

Saving Jobs

Whatever knowledge today's, or tomorrow's, worker brings to the job or has acquired on it, the likelihood is that it will not be an adequate guarantee of employment security. Changes that no individual can control—the development of new technologies, the closing of old plants—require community responses. City and state governments, business, and organized labor will all have to collaborate, as they already do in some places, to handle the inevitable dislocations.

We have become sadly familiar with the damage done to communities where a major employer closes up shop, leaving workers jobless and the tax base depleted. The fabric of municipal life—schools, roads, utilities, services—remains to be financed and used, but the activity which sustained that infrastructure disappears. What is left is an expensive shell and a sense of helplessness.

We are less familiar with the variety of responses Americans have developed to prevent unnecessary plant closings or to cushion the impact of shutdowns that cannot be avoided. Pointing the way toward the kind of public-private partnerships that must be more widely adopted, these local answers to a problem that is genuinely national illustrate some of our options for cooperation.

One form of partnership is the Area Labor-Management Committee, twenty of which have been created around the country. The Jamestown, New York, ALMC is a good example of how they work. In the early 1970s, Jamestown was a typical aging, depressed Frostbelt community. As old industries failed and new ones went elsewhere, labor-management conflict intensified. The parties only stopped fighting when a plant closing cost 700 jobs and provoked the formation of the Jamestown Area Labor-Management Committee to form a common front against economic decay. The results have been spectacular.

In ten years of continuous operation, this committee composed of labor, management, and government members has not only saved 800 existing jobs, but brought in nearly 1,500 new ones. Labor relations, measured by production days lost through work stoppages, improved dramatically. Worker participation has increased overall productivity and innovation. And the program has not required large dollar contributions from government or the private sector.

In other communities, employees have been able to buy out management and become their own bosses. About sixty firms threatened with shutdowns in the 1970s took this route to survival, an option that saved at least 50,000 jobs and led to only three failures among the new firms.

In other cases workers and managers negotiated tradeoffs—stock ownership instead of wage or benefit increases, greater employee involvement in decision making—as bargains to keep companies viable. In Philadelphia, for instance, the union at A & P supermarkets agreed to concessions on wage and vacation pay in exchange for the reopening of at least twenty A & P stores as Super Fresh Food Centers. The contract, moreover, gave the union the first right to buy certain stores at fair market value and provided for comprehensive labor-management problem solving to improve store profits.

A third option—conversion to a new product line—was taken by International Silver in its Meriden, Connecticut, plant. The company shifted out of its stainless steel operation into three new businesses, using funds available under the Federal Trade Readjustment Act to retrain its workers as toolmakers.

Aiding Displaced Workers

Such success stories do not remove the possibility of displacement and the need for a combination of federal, state, business, and union programs to aid displaced workers. The most effective help, again, comes from local initiatives delivered promptly at low cost.

The California Economic Adjustment Team (CEAT) is one such program. Responding to a 1980–1981 crisis, in the course of which it was shown that most workers in the state's five hardest-hit industries lacked transferable skills, CEAT created fourteen large reemployment centers offering comprehensive adjustment assistance to nearly 30,000 displaced workers.

When the Mack truck plant in Hayward, California, closed, for example, the CEAT technique played a part in the formation of a local assistance and placement center to survey the skills and needs of the Mack workers, develop programs enabling them to transfer their skills, and provide them with information on available community services. This joint business, union, and municipal project also helped sponsor a mini–job fair for women at UAW Local 76, convinced a bank to contribute the services of loan experts for credit and mortgage counseling, and persuaded the Hayward Private Industry Council to contract with Local 76 for twenty-eight on-the-job training positions.

Michigan, another state severely hurt by plant closings, has seen the development of a model private-sector adjustment program through the Downriver Community Conference. Its Economic Readjustment Program, administered by a nonprofit agency using federal funds, has concentrated on treating potential employers in and out of the area as customers for a product: skilled or retrained workers. Maintaining steady contact with employers to determine their actual or projected needs, the program placed approximately 70 percent of its worker participants in new jobs during its first phase, July 1980 through October 1981.

These examples teach two important lessons. The sooner help comes, the more effective it can be. The closer the collaboration among business, labor, and the community, the better off all of them are.

But local responses cannot completely solve a national problem. It is the legitimate responsibility of the federal government to ensure that a comprehensive system is in place so that the displaced worker has somewhere to turn when cast adrift. Federal assistance is also required, both in cash and in services, to aid

workers searching for jobs (the least expensive activity) or training for new ones (the most expensive).

While unemployment insurance payments can reach $160 a
week, federal help can be delivered as information on job availability or as assistance in adaptation to new jobs for well under
$100 per recipient. Expansion of the Job Service Matching Sys-
tem—a computerized data bank that lists applicants best qualified
against job orders on file—and of the system of job clubs can
make two useful services even more effective.

For some workers relocation is the best option, but one they
can only take if some of their moving costs are offset by federal
subsidies. Aside from assisting with such expenses, however,
federal information programs should also be improved to help job
hunters know the prospects in different, distant labor markets
and narrow their search to the most promising potential openings.

Training for the Future

Over the next decade, American workers will face a substantial
occupational upheaval. Many of today's occupations will be substantially altered or simply will no longer exist. Workers from
shop floor to office will need new skills to work with emerging
information technologies.

Experienced workers who lose their jobs in traditional manufacturing industries are increasingly finding they have the wrong
skills for new employment. Yet there is almost no federal effort
to help these workers in transition.

Our employment and training institutions are, by and large,
unprepared to assist American workers in making the massive
adjustments that lie ahead. Not only is government funding for
basic education, training, and retraining now falling far short of
what is needed, we don't have the data to identify projected jobs
or match available workers with available jobs. There is no na-

tional job register or means of forecasting the kinds of jobs we'll need in the future. We have no system to evaluate the success and cost of different approaches to training, nor an information network along which to communicate innovations in training techniques or experiences even in neighboring states. There is little cooperation among public and private programs—or even among the various public programs. The results—duplication, omission, fragmentation, and waste.

The most productive role government can play is to supply leadership for and promote contact among the three agents that bear the basic responsibility for action: America's schools, employers, and unions. But government leadership in coordinating the national effort is nearly nonexistent now. It must be far stronger.

First, we must have the programs and funding in place to make sure all workers can get the education and training they need to make themselves employable. Government funding for basic education, training, and retraining now falls short of what is needed. Actually, the amount needed is not that large. We could fully fund the three main types of government training assistance—vocational, on-the-job, and higher-education retraining—for between $103 million and $717 million a year, depending on the qualifications established for recipients.

Second, we should consider reforms of the unemployment insurance program. Two promising possibilities are allowing unemployed workers to continue to collect unemployment insurance beyond the set period if they are enrolled in a state-certified education or training program for an occupation in high demand; and allowing employees, whose work hours are temporarily reduced to avoid layoffs, to receive partial unemployment insurance benefits.

Finally, we need to look at real reform: a comprehensive strategy for training that leads to private-sector employment and provides financial support during the transition. If we do so, then the occupational upheaval could bring new opportunities for displaced workers, as well as for women and minority workers who have been underrepresented in traditional occupations.

SAVING FOR TRAINING Two models of broad reform have been proposed. One is called the Individual Training Account (ITA), analogous to the popular Individual Retirement Account (IRA).

The idea, which originated with economist Pat Choate of TRW, is to create personal job-training and relocation funds for employees against the time when they will need to acquire new skills. Funds would be contributed to the ITA by both workers and employers, with each making annual, tax-deductible payments of $300 to $500 (or more) until the total reached $6,000. The account would then be available to a worker to spend on retraining or relocation. If the need arose before the account reached its maximum, or if training was needed for someone just entering the work force, the ITA could provide advances from reserves up to the amount the worker would eventually contribute from future earnings. Since, from the start, contributions by men and women already at work would build up ITA reserves rapidly, the advances should not require any federal funds.

Indeed, beyond the tax deduction and the initial legislation establishing this as a national system, the federal role would be small. The only limit on the worker's choice of a training or retraining facility would be the requirement, similar to that of the GI Bill, that the training institution be certified by the Labor Department as offering an acceptable quality of instruction. Like IRAs and other saving incentives, these accounts should retain their favorable tax treatment under any proposed tax reforms.

This saving-for-training system would give workers wide freedom to choose the skills they want to learn and the place where they put them to use. It would also give them the flexibility to take their ITA contributions, with interest, directly to a new job if they so chose or to remove their share of the fund (but not the employer's) when they retired. The amount withdrawn would only be taxed as income when spent, at a time when other earnings will presumably be low or nonexistent.

An ITA mechanism, in sum, would add a valuable set of incentives to traditional job-training programs. It would give the workers a direct interest in and control over their own future. Companies would have concrete incentives to retrain workers rather than laying them off.

Simple to understand and to administer, the ITA would not require direct government subsidies or high administrative costs. Establishing it would reduce pressure on unemployment insurance funds. And putting ITA money to use in an economic downturn should operate as a countercyclical stimulus to recovery as well as a vital source of support for training and retraining.

Another model of reform has been offered by Roger Vaughan, senior fellow of the Gallatin Institute. He has proposed a type of GI Bill for the work force that would provide all workers—employed and unemployed—with access to education and training vouchers.

Mr. Vaughan's concept is somewhat similar to the Individual Training Account, but it is wider-ranging. It would put special emphasis on those groups most in need of such services: the disadvantaged and unskilled population and the working poor. At the same time, it would also serve displaced workers and middle-income workers in need of retraining.

The GI Bill is a good model, for it enabled millions of Americans to gain the education needed to become productive members of the work force at a comparatively low cost. Mr. Vaughan's idea, building on this type of system, is to replace the current cumbersome system of numerous education, training, and retraining programs with one simple system which will ensure that people will have the money to get the type of training, retraining, or continuing education they need.

Funding for this system would be primarily through a 2 percent tax on gross annual wages for all employees (with the first

$5,000 excluded)—1 percent paid by the employer and 1 percent by the employee. The revenues would flow directly into trust funds established at the state level. Since this system would replace existing federal and state employment training programs, the tax could be offset with a partial credit against income taxes for both employers and employees.

Individuals would accumulate credits toward their personal voucher—up to a maximum value of $3,000—in a variety of ways. For the employed, the credit would be earned on a monthly basis, starting at $50 for those making under $10,000 annually, and declining to $5 for those making over $30,000. The unemployed would receive a $50 credit for each month they are unemployed and drawing unemployment insurance benefits. Recipients of Aid to Families with Dependent Children who are employable and entrants to the labor market from low-income households would be eligible for a voucher of $2,500. This advanced voucher would be "repaid" by the recipients' earning no additional credits during their first three years of work.

INDUSTRY INITIATIVES American industry has the human and technical resources and, above all, the self-interest to achieve the best results in training and retraining. It already spends about $30 billion a year on equipping workers with new skills. Since it should bear the lion's share of worker training and retraining in the future it may well have to spend more. It will certainly have to spend better.

What industry needs, aside from modest government assistance and extensive labor cooperation, is to find the best techniques with the least duplication of effort. There are many models.

General Electric's experience in compressing the education of a machinist for jet engine parts from three years to six months shows what the application of technology to instruction can accomplish. Another company—Control Data Corporation of Minneapolis—has pioneered in efforts to boost productivity through training and retraining.

I had the chance in July 1982 to talk to William Norris, the Control Data chairman who built a multimillion-dollar operation from a one-man business. As we sat in my Washington office, Norris spoke quietly, modestly, about both the effort he had helped launch and the research effort needed to keep it moving. What came through to me most strongly was his certainty that industry bears the primary responsibility for creating the skilled work force America must have, but that the job also requires an effective partnership with government.

Control Data has already done a great deal by and for itself. Using its own technology, for example, it developed the PLATO computer-based courses for on-the-job training through a companywide system of television, audio and video tapes, and telephone and satellite transmission. PLATO has proved so cost effective a method that universities, foundations, and other companies have joined Control Data in cooperative projects affecting thousands of workers. As the centerpiece of Control Data's own Fair Break program to train the disadvantaged, the PLATO system reaches people at fifty centers around the United States, with training in basic skills as well as guidance for job seekers and help in managing personal finances. In cooperation with public schools, Fair Break takes people from behind the occupational eight ball to give them a crucial, clear shot at finding and keeping a job.

Control Data, in a consortium with ten other companies and two church organizations known as City Venture, has also gone into the business of fighting urban decay through job creation and training. City Venture has had its successes and failures. It has apparently begun to turn around the blighted Warren-Sherman neighborhood in Toledo, Ohio. A commitment of $7.5 million in public funds has generated $30 million more in private financing aimed at revitalizing business and industry—large and small— in the community and creating 2,000 new jobs. "Warren-Sherman," says William Norris, "shows that public funds, if effectively targeted, can lead to large private commitments."

His company's commitment and range of creative activities provide a model others can follow. It is not the only model, and it is not only for industry. The model works best when it employs both public and private resources. For that kind of cooperation to spread and succeed, government at all levels must do more, not just to fund programs with seed money but also, as a catalytic agent, to bring industry, labor, and communities together for unified, effective action.

LABOR'S CONTRIBUTION The need for such a concerted approach to training and retraining workers is too broad to be answered without the help of organized labor. What the other sectors contribute in resources and experience, labor can match in its unique ability to reach out to workers themselves, to potential trainees.

To fill this important role, unions must overcome the tendency to assume that adding skills means losing members. In the early years of the Information Revolution, it is true that service and high-technology workers were not brought into the organized labor movement. The demand for skilled technicians was such that individuals with the requisite abilities did not need union protection. But training will increase the numbers of qualified applicants for such jobs and, as supply and demand come more nearly into balance, the need for unions to protect workers will also rise. Unions owe it to themselves and to their present and future members to become part of the solution now.

One New York local—District 1199 of the National Union of Hospital and Health Care Employees—perceived the need and the opportunity early. The District 1199 Training and Upgrading Fund has exemplified the outreach potential of unions since it was created in 1969.

Financed by approximately 1 percent of the members' gross payroll, the fund set up its own educational programs. They range from courses leading to a high school diploma, to full-time instruction in X-ray, respiration-therapy, and lab technology. More members apply than the fund is able to support.

March 1982 brought a different kind of breakthrough in a

much more beleaguered field. Six months after the Ford Motor Company and the United Auto Workers concluded their new contract, the union opened a million-dollar National Development and Training Center in Dearborn, Michigan, with the goal of retraining 45,000 workers Ford had laid off.

The center is precedent setting. The bill for it is to be paid by a deduction of five cents an hour from each Ford-UAW worker's wages. The services it offers include career counseling and guidance as well as job search and placement help. A national vocational retraining assistance plan will provide workers with five years' seniority or more up to $1,000 toward tuition, and full-time courses of vocational instruction will be targeted on jobs that have already been identified.

These examples give a measure of the potential contribution organized labor can make to a national partnership for productivity. They also show the beginnings of labor's response to a challenge that affects union interests as much as those of industry. They only hint at the potential of establishing a larger framework for cooperation.

Ensuring Equity in Pay

One other employment issue, however, requires prompt government action: ensuring that women in the work force receive comparable pay for doing work of comparable worth. The fight for this essential guarantee of equity in the workplace is being fought—and won—in the states. Thirteen of them now have statutes assuring equal pay for work comparable in "worth" or "character." But the federal government, as the nation's largest employer, must show leadership in the struggle so the private sector comes to see pay equity as a just and accepted practice to be implemented fully.

For generations, women have invested their talents, resources, and energies in the American economy. Today, more than half the women over sixteen are in the labor force. They are carrying large economic responsibilities: 74 percent of them are single, separated, divorced, widowed, or living with a man who earns less than $15,000 a year.

But the returns for women's work have been slim: 60 percent of women employed full time earn less than $10,000 a year and 50 percent of poor households are headed by women. In the past thirty years, the number of women in the labor force doubled, while the number of men increased by one quarter. At the same time, however, there has been little change in the ratio of women's earnings to men's. In 1955 women working full time earned, on the average, 64 percent of what men earned; by 1981, women's earnings had dropped to 59 percent of men's.

Although the Equal Pay Act of 1963 requires employers to pay the same wages to both sexes for substantially equal work, women continue to earn less than men performing the same work. For example, the April 1982 *Monthly Labor Review* states that "the median weekly earnings for women in sales were only 52 percent of those for men in the same field." A female clerical worker earns 60 percent of what her male counterpart receives. Women accountants earn only 72 percent of what men earn; women craft workers are paid 67 percent of the men's earnings; and female college professors receive 71 percent of what is earned by their male colleagues.

Substantial differences between men's and women's pay can be found even in job classes where female workers are in the majority. For example, women account for about 68 percent of the elementary and secondary school teachers, but their median wage is about 83 percent of the men's median wage. While 91 percent of the registered nurses, dieticians, and therapists are women, they still earn only 95 percent of what men performing the same work receive.

These unfortunate statistics exist despite enactment of the Equal Pay Act of 1963 and the Civil Rights Act of 1964, which made wage discrimination illegal and essentially mandated equal pay for equal work in the same workplace.

But the fact is, the vast majority of women don't work at the same jobs as men. This occupational segregation is the largest contributor to the disparity between the earnings of men and women. When women in traditionally female classifications do work that requires equal or greater skill, knowledge, education, experience, and responsibility compared to the tasks performed by men with different jobs, they are too often paid less.

Specifically, women are substantially more likely than men to work in clerical and service occupations and less likely to work in craft and laboring occupations. The Department of Labor found that 80 percent of women in the work force in 1980 were in clerical, sales, service, or plant jobs. These jobs tend to be low paying when compared to those held predominantly by males.

Consider the following examples: in Montgomery County, Maryland, a liquor store clerk with a high school diploma and two years of experience earns $12,479 a year. Yet a schoolteacher in the same county, with a bachelor's degree and two years of experience, receives $12,323 a year. While almost all the liquor clerks are male, two thirds of the county's schoolteachers are female.

A November 1980 study in San Jose, California, showed the monthly salary of a beginning librarian was $750 a month while a street-sweeper operator earned $758.

And in my own state of Colorado, nurses earned monthly starting salaries of $1,064, compared with male tree trimmers and painters, who earned $1,164 and $1,191 a month respectively.

These disparities are discriminatory. They have been outlawed in principle. They should be eliminated in practice.

The federal government can begin with two steps. First it should design a bias-free evaluation system for classifying the 2.1 million federal employees.

Second, the Equal Employment Opportunity Commission and the Office of Federal Contract Compliance Programs should perform extensive research into the reasons the wages of females in the work force are depressed. They should eliminate all discrimination in compensation, including wages for different jobs that require comparable experience, education, responsibility, and so on.

Women are entering the labor force in unprecedented numbers, primarily to maintain their family's standard of living. Simple justice dictates that they be compensated on an equitable basis. There can be no economic equality for women without the principle of equal pay for work of comparable worth.

More Than a Paycheck

Most imagination in reforming and modernizing the work force will not come from government. Bureaucracies are designed to administer, not innovate. And already the most innovative answers to Americans' questions about the future of work are being developed by the workers themselves. They are the most hopeful signs of our ability to profit from change.

The variety of new approaches to work reflects the human realization that a job means more than a paycheck. America's affluence—even though not yet completely secure or equitable—has altered the meaning of work for many of us. It is no longer the core around which all life revolves. What has become important, along with the financial reward a job brings, is the psychic payoff, the quality of work as part of the quality of life.

Americans seek and are obtaining a greater share in managing the enterprises where they spend nearly half their waking hours. They are finding ways to adjust those hours, as well, to conform to their preferences as well as their employers' needs. And they are finding a new role for themselves on the job, the satisfaction of using their intellect for productivity as well as for production.

These changes in the organization and management of work not only meet millions of Americans' real needs and desires; they can also boost productivity in the future. New technologies and recent changes in the nature of work and the workplace have given many workers increased discretion over their own performance on the job. New ways of looking at work and new roles for workers can raise morale, reduce turnover and absenteeism, and increase creativity, all of which contribute to improving productivity.

Cooperation, companies all over the country are discovering, is both a more effective and a more profitable management tool than confrontation. Employees are becoming partners instead of replaceable extensions of the machines they operate. This change responds to workers' need to feel that they have some control over their economic future. It is fueled by an old American character trait, self-reliance, and it is promoting a healthy return to individual responsibility.

The challenge we face here is a fresh one, and it is full of creative potential: to design and implement new workplace practices and labor market strategies, giving greater freedom of choice to people regarding both their life on the job and how the job fits into their total life pattern. The innovative possibilities—in such categories as worker participation, employee ownership, and flexible work schedules—are endless. They stem from America's reservoir of inventiveness, and they require a minimum of government encouragement, but a maximum of individual ingenuity.

HAVING A SAY AT THE WORKPLACE Last spring, in a cramped room off the shop floor of Cleveland's TRW company, I sat in on a small part of the revolution in the workplace. Around a plain rectangular table, about a dozen workers and a shop foreman bent over mimeographed sheets of statistics on the flow of products and the rate of productivity of their section of the giant firm. I was a guest, and a silent one, at this regular midmorning session of the work quality circle, and my presence did not seem to inhibit the spirited give-and-take among its members, men and women, black and white, as they talked their way through an agenda chalked up on the blackboard that was the room's only decoration.

These factory workers were turning themselves into management consultants. Their circle was analyzing data on problems and opportunities in the production process, debating alternative methods, and preparing to report the findings to their employer. That was the surface level of their activity. What counted as much as their analysis was their involvement, the recognition being given to their knowledge and talent, the reward to them in self-fulfillment.

Thousands of such work quality circles have come to life around the country. Though they were first established in manufacturing, they are applicable to service industries as well. They are spreading throughout white-collar ranks, including engineering staffs and middle management. Not all quality circles have survived. Those that have died were usually put together too hurriedly and too narrowly. Those that were carefully developed and integrated into the operation of the company have not only survived but thrived, illustrating their considerable potential for the worker and for management.

Quality circles are actually part of a broader phenomenon known as the quality of work life (QWL) movement. While QWL means different things to different people, it basically encompasses all forms of direct participation by workers in day-to-day decision making on the job. It is based, first and foremost, on a cooperative, problem-solving relationship between labor and management, instead of the familiar adversarial style.

The QWL movement has grown rapidly from its beginnings just a decade ago. QWL programs got an early boost from General Motors, which started with voluntary activities in 1973 but required them for all operating units within a few years. The steel industry established labor-management participation teams under a 1980 contract, and at Jones and Laughlin Steel and National Steel, workers have been volunteering for team membership faster than they can be absorbed. National Steel, in fact, put its initial experimental program on a companywide basis after saving $800,000 through worker participation at one of its Indiana divisions.

QWL's current popularity is demonstrated by the fact that some 900 union, company, and government officials convened in late 1982 for the first nationally sponsored conference on labor-management cooperation.

Worker participation is an experiment worth continuing and expanding, but with some caution and a clear sense of its limitations. QWL programs, based on cooperative labor-management relations, should stay separate from collective-bargaining activities. They should emphasize protection of workers' rights—especially job security and voluntary participation—as much as higher productivity. The benefits they bring should be shared with fairness so that the tangible results that employers register are matched by the intangible results that workers get from being treated with dignity and having a voice in shaping their jobs.

"Worker participation," says Glenn Watts, president of the Communications Workers of America, "is a new issue for the 1980s. . . . Changes in the economic and social scene challenge us to develop new approaches. Collective bargaining, in its traditional version, is not enough to keep pace with the rapid changes which face us. The labor movement must add new skills and strategies to affect the planning of the future."

Some modest actions by government can ease and encourage this healthy process. To help the growth of QWL programs, for instance, the federal Mediation and Conciliation Service could provide new services to assist unions and management with information, technical advice, and finding a setting for cooperation. Where existing laws inhibit worker participation, those laws should be changed.

A PIECE OF THE ACTION Perhaps the ultimate expression of workers' participation is ownership. In the last few years, 3 million to 4 million workers have become stockholders for the first time through the approximately 5,000 employee stock ownership plans (ESOPs) in existence.

The rewards are more than psychic. A Southern retail lumber and hardware enterprise, Lowe's Companies, has found that having 6,000 employees as owners of most of the stock spurred sales per worker to three times the average of such national chains as K mart, J. C. Penney, and Sears, Roebuck. At another seventy-five companies with ESOPs, one study showed, there was a 157 percent average increase in net profits three years after a plan's establishment.

The advantages of employee ownership are not limited to financial balance sheets. Without stripping management of control, these plans enlarge workers' stake in an enterprise, saving jobs and raising productivity, from which the employees realize direct benefits. ESOPs also enhance capital formation and broaden the distribution of wealth. They have developed without much government help, but they could be spread further if companies were obliged by new legislation to create such plans to qualify for such special-preference federal programs as export subsidies, small-business loans, and the tax forgiveness likely to be central to new enterprise-zone initiatives.

WINDING DOWN THE TIME CLOCK Another strategy that is proving both popular and effective—and that should be encouraged—is the introduction of flexible work hours. Scheduling that better suits workers' needs is not just the momentary whim of a leisure-obsessed society. It is the logical and reasonable consequence of a changing labor force, one in which women with children, as well as the elderly, play increasingly prominent parts. As individuals and as groups they seek both greater convenience and better treatment at work. Flexible hours (flextime) and part-time work offer them—but not them only—wider opportunities in the labor market, while giving employers a broader range of skilled personnel to hire.

Flextime originated in Europe in the mid-1960s and crossed the Atlantic within about five years. Control Data, to cite one among many examples, uses it for three quarters of its more than 60,000 employees, allowing them to choose the times they report for and leave work as long as they work the same number of hours every day and their scheduling does not disrupt the work flow. After two years the company found lateness had dropped by nearly half and sick leave by 16 percent.

Another method of relieving conflicts between competing job and personal demands—and, sometimes, increasing productivity—is to make part-time work more respectable and rewarding. Today our 15 million part-time workers in nonagricultural industries, including one quarter of all working women, are often made to feel like second-class hired help. Low pay and poor benefits characterize their treatment. Many have to choose between staying home or taking full-time jobs, which require them to put their children's care in the hands of others.

There is no reason to bind ourselves to such limited alternatives. Part-time workers are too productive a resource to waste, when skills are in short supply and two people sharing a full-time job can often do more than the work of one. Such arrangements should be encouraged by concentrating on job security, fair treatment, and the development of wider opportunities for part-timers and job sharers.

Flextime was endorsed by Congress in 1982 for federal employees and deserves presidential encouragement, largely through jawboning. More substantively, we should move to amend the Fair Labor Standards Act to provide prorated fringe and unemployment insurance benefits for part-time work.

CONTINUING EDUCATION The standard progression of our lives, from education through employment to retirement and inactivity, is being challenged as Americans come to see life not in terms of successive conditions, but as a continuum in which work and leisure can alternate productively and education continues throughout.

Explosive changes in technology and management techniques make continuing education essential. Improved medicine and health have greatly reduced both the need and the desire for a fallow old age. And we have discovered how much creative leisure can enrich family life and lighten the pressures of modern mass society.

There is no reason not to put more flexibility into the patterns created in other times. When teachers, artists, lawyers, and other senior professionals take a leave of absence to renew their skills and refresh their energies, we call their time off a sabbatical. The concept could and should be extended to give other kinds of employees a six- to twelve-month leave after seven or ten years on the job, in order to prepare for a second career, to acquire fresh knowledge for use in a current job, or just to ease the transition from work to retirement.

Such breaks could come in stages for workers in their thirties, fifties, and sixties, either as formal educational programs or as less-structured opportunities to get a second wind. Such opportunities, whatever their immediate benefits in reduced unemployment and improved training and morale, would significantly elevate the quality of working life. More frequent transitions would bring smoother transitions—from school to work, from work to retirement.

To widen the use of sabbaticals, we could consider permitting workers to take a year or two of retirement benefits ahead of time, a way of making such leaves of absence financially practicable for the individual and for industry.

The pressures for such changes to make life and work richer are gathering force. The challenge to government is to smooth the way where it can, allowing transformation to come with less disruption, so that as our horizons expand, the ground beneath our feet holds firm.

The new employment strategy outlined in this chapter goes well beyond the familiar territory of the past. In an increasingly technological age, brain power will be vastly more important than muscle power. This means our national employment strategy must consider both the type of education our children are receiving and every kind of workplace innovation that can increase our job satisfaction and productivity.

It all boils down to a return to basics:

- An education that will prepare our children for meeting the demands of a new labor market and for making thoughtful, informed judgments in an increasingly technological society
- A training and retraining system that will help workers keep their skills up to date and provide adjustment assistance when needed
- A workplace that gives the worker a sense of dignity and fulfillment on the job

In short, investing in people—in their education, their training, their productivity, and their fulfillment—must become the focus for our strategy in the 1980s. It will be critical to the long-run economic health of this country.

PART II

—•—

National Security Today and Tomorrow

PERSPECTIVE ON A CHANGING WORLD

———◆———

*Weapons are of little use on
the field of battle if there is
no wise counsel at home.*

—CICERO

In the decades since our military requirements were last the subject of sustained and comprehensive review the world has changed dramatically. Regrettably, our defense structure has not kept pace with this transformation.

The greatest quantitative change since the early 1960s is the growth in the number of nuclear weapons, not only in the American and Soviet arsenals but also in those of so-called medium powers like France and China. Worse, the number of nuclear powers is growing. India joined the nuclear club in 1974 and other countries can be expected to follow suit by the end of this decade. Nor is there reason to believe we can long escape a new nightmare, the implications of which we have not yet begun to fathom: nuclear weapons in the hands of "pariah states" or terrorists.

Today, our ability to fashion and implement an effective military policy is inextricably linked to the subject of nuclear arms control. Any national security policy that does not assign top priority to preventing the use of nuclear weapons is not only irresponsible but, ultimately, immoral.

A second great change is the increase in Soviet military power, conventional as well as nuclear. The single most dramatic development has been the expansion of the Soviet Navy from a coastal defense force to a true blue-water fleet. Today, Soviet aircraft carriers roam both the Pacific and the Atlantic; supersonic "Backfire" bombers threaten our surface forces with powerful anti-ship missiles; and, most dangerous of all, the Soviet submarine force is not only three times the size of our own but may be our equal in quality.

Third, we are in the midst of a revolution in the world balance of power. Thirty years ago, there were really only two major powers in the world—the United States and the USSR. Today, there are many. France, Britain, and China have nuclear weapons and many other states have powerful conventional forces. Even small nations have the option of protracted guerrilla warfare against a superpower invader—as the Afghans have shown the Russians. This shift in relative power is potentially even more important than changes in the Soviet-American military balance. We must be in a position to meet whatever challenges the new distribution of power may present.

Finally, twenty years ago we were not dependent on foreign sources of energy. Today we are. As much as we would like to ignore it, the problem of our reliance on imported oil for the lifeblood of our economy will not disappear. Our nation has been fortunate so far in avoiding the worst conceivable cost of our dependence on foreign energy supplies: we haven't gone to war in the Middle East. But the threat remains very real. Although the oil glut of 1982 may have removed it from our daily consciousness, it remains just over the horizon.

Our addiction to foreign oil could be every bit as damaging to our military and economic security as a Soviet ultimatum. Nothing would do more to guarantee the preservation of our national sovereignty, and to prove that free people can determine their own fate, than for us to reduce the amount of oil we buy abroad and to maintain imports at levels tolerable for our security and independence.

Policies that do not take into account these four basic changes are bound to fail. Furthermore, these challenges cannot be adequately answered by throwing money at a defense establishment created to meet the military needs of the past. Increased military spending does not automatically buy us greater security. The argument that more spending on defense is better is no more valid than the old argument that less spending is better. Only better is better.

What does better mean in defense?

Better means an intelligent definition of our security interests and the specific military strategy necessary to protect them.

Better means selecting weapons to implement that strategy, instead of giving every defense interest its customary bureaucratic slice of the pie.

Better means exploiting innovative military concepts and technologies. Too often, the ease and bureaucratic safety of following routine make significant innovation impossible.

Better means focusing not just on management efficiency in the Defense Department but also on battlefield effectiveness.

Better means advancement of the most creative and imaginative officers, people with an understanding of warfare.

There is one other step we must take—a step of at least equal importance to our common defense, but of a slightly different nature. An effective military is not just equipment, nor a combination of equipment with strategy and tactics. It is, most importantly, people. The best equipment and doctrine in the world will not help a military that has lost its morale. We must restore pride to our services.

In this section, I propose some specific steps for creating an effective and affordable defense for the 1980s and 1990s. While they are not all inclusive, the chapters that follow do attempt to address the three areas where new thinking is needed most: the development of a military strategy that meets today's needs and the reform of our armed forces to ensure we can carry it out, a plan for reducing our dangerous dependence on foreign oil so we will never be tempted to go to war for it, and a comprehensive approach to controlling the nuclear arms race.

The list of what we need to do to ensure our common defense in the 1980s is formidable and varied. But these steps, taken together or in any combination, will not be sufficient if we are unable to take one additional, even more fundamental step: the reestablishment of domestic consensus.

However great the number and effectiveness of the weapons we amass, however high the morale of our troops, however shrewd our diplomacy, however advantageous our arms control policy, they will not make our nation secure unless we have the requisite consensus to defend our values, our interests, our homeland, and our fellow Americans. The steps outlined in this section are designed to help us bestow that sense of purpose and national will.

TOWARD A MORE EFFECTIVE DEFENSE

———◆———

*The result of a battle is decided not by the
orders of a commander-in-chief,
nor by the place where the troops are stationed,
nor by the cannon or of
slaughtered men, but by that intangible force
called the spirit of the army.*

—TOLSTOY

The defense issues that absorb most of our time and attention today are not those that history tells us are most important. Fashioning an effective military policy for the 1980s and 1990s requires a great debate. But, in large part, our national defense debate has deteriorated into a shallow and stylized shouting match over very limited and increasingly irrelevant issues. Noisy arguments take place over the size or growth rate of the defense budget, over specific treaty commitments, and over certain major weapons. But larger questions, such as strategy and military doctrine, are seldom considered.

During a chance meeting in the 1930s between the French Popular Front premier, Léon Blum, and Charles de Gaulle, then a young colonel, De Gaulle reportedly reproached Blum about the state of France's defenses. Blum replied angrily: "But we are spending more for defense than the previous government!" De

Gaulle pleaded, "It is what you are spending it for that I want to discuss." Blum dismissed him with the words "I leave that to the generals." These same generals were pouring billions of francs into the ill-fated Maginot Line.

A typical congressional defense debate today is all too suggestive of the French debate in the 1930s. The French politicians argued furiously over how much to spend on the Maginot Line. But few asked whether the Maginot Line reflected a correct strategy, or whether it would actually work in combat in the face of Germany's panzer divisions.

We have to broaden the debate. New ideas and reforms are needed on two levels. First, we need a new military strategy that is relevant to today's challenges. Second, we must undertake military reform so that if conflicts occur, our conventional forces will prevail.

Renewing Our Strategy

If we are to have an effective defense, it is essential that we begin to develop a new military strategy and to procure the appropriate military forces. In this connection, our first priority must be the restoration of United States naval superiority.

Few American policy makers dispute the desirability of control of the world's oceans. Yet today, we no longer have the clear-cut naval supremacy we enjoyed in the late 1940s. It is easy to see what happened.

Shortly after the Second World War, the United States made a major commitment to defend the European continent from the Soviet Army. It was an appropriate commitment at the time. The European nations, victors and vanquished alike, were exhausted.

At that time, we had maritime superiority by default, guaranteed by the immense navy left over from World War II. The Soviet Navy, while nominally strong in submarines, had performed poorly in the war, was technically backward, and had virtually no capabilities beyond Soviet coastal waters.

Today, the situation has changed drastically. Far from being weak and poor, the European nations are strong and wealthy. Western Europe collectively has a larger population than either the United States or the USSR. Its total economic output is greater than that of the United States or the entire Warsaw Pact. NATO Europe has about 3.2 million men under arms. This is nearly 2 million less than the Warsaw Pact nations (including the Soviet Union), but the NATO countries have neither the Pact's problems of potential unreliability (such as in Poland and Rumania) nor that of geographic dispersion (one quarter of the Soviet Army is stationed along the Chinese border). Two of our European allies, Britain and France, have their own nuclear deterrents.

At sea, the situation has also changed. In the past two decades, the Soviet Union has mounted a major naval challenge, the greatest challenge by a continental power to a traditionally dominant sea power since Admiral Alfred von Tirpitz built the German High Seas Fleet to challenge Britain early in this century.

During the 1960s and early 1970s, while the Soviets were investing massively in warships, most American defense dollars were going into the Vietnam War. We retired large numbers of ships that had reached the end of their service life. Between 1964 and 1975, our active fleet shrank from 859 ships to 475. The carrier force, the backbone of our surface fleet, declined from 23 ships to only 13.

We are now called upon to respond to this major naval challenge with our naval capital diminished. We must make reestablishing and maintaining naval supremacy the first priority for our conventional forces. In other words, we must adopt a maritime strategy.

The logic behind a maritime strategy is compelling. First, despite our important relationships with Canada and Mexico, we are essentially an island nation. Our trade in raw materials moves by sea. The importance of control of the sea is growing, not diminishing, as world economic interdependence grows.

Second, obvious and indisputable American naval superiority

would sharply limit Soviet military and diplomatic options in dealing with third-world nations. Although the Soviet Union can influence nations on her border without using the sea (for example, Afghanistan), most of the areas where the Soviets are seeking or are likely to seek influence—Africa, Southeast Asia, even much of the Middle East—are not accessible overland from the USSR. To a large extent, the Soviets' ability to project force abroad depends on their unhampered use of the sea.

Finally, the defense of important American allies in Europe and Asia requires United States naval superiority. If the American fleet is not adequate to confront Soviet naval squadrons in the Indian Ocean, or off the Horn of Africa, or in Southeast Asia, allied as well as American trade routes and access to resources could be threatened.

The West as a whole has vital interests far beyond the European continent. British activity in the Persian Gulf, French actions in Africa, and increasing economic ties between the European nations and Saudi Arabia are all evidence of this. Far more than the United States, our closest allies depend on seaborne imports and exports. Just in petroleum, while we import 37.4 percent of our oil needs, Japan imports 98.1 percent, Germany 97.7 percent, France 100 percent, and Italy 100 percent. Nor is oil the whole story. France, for example, imports 75 percent of its total energy needs, plus all of its cobalt, manganese, platinum, and titanium sponge—raw materials vital to its modern, industrial economy. The French Ministry of Industry estimates that a six-month to one-year interruption of oil supplies just from the Middle East—not from all of OPEC—would cripple the French economy.

As a result, the growth of Soviet naval power threatens European vital interests as much as ours. Unfortunately, only France and Britain have any significant ability to defend their interests outside Europe.

Recognizing that the West's joint interests extend beyond national borders suggests a need for rethinking the division of labor within NATO. Just as the West has worldwide interests, so it has worldwide defense needs. A maritime strategy would require the United States to be able to mount a more effective sea and air defense of the West's lifelines in the Atlantic and Pacific. Since we could not afford to do that while maintaining our army in Europe at its present size, NATO nations then would have to assume—over a period of time and by collective plan and agreement—a proportionately greater share of the land defense of the Continent itself.

Europe may not yet have the desire to take greater responsibility for its own land defenses. But it has the potential to do so; it has the population and the wealth. And beyond that, it has the need. The price of continued high American land defense expenditures in Europe would be our diminished ability to defend the West's interests elsewhere, particularly at sea. This price is unacceptable to both Europeans and Americans. Our political leadership must make that increasingly clear.

Our political leaders must also be prepared to build the kind of navy a maritime strategy requires. That is a different navy from the one proposed by the Reagan Administration. We need to build very different types of ships from those we are building today. The big nuclear carrier is becoming obsolete. As the Falklands war showed, we live in a time when every surface ship is growing more and more vulnerable. Worse, the carriers are increasingly irrelevant to the Soviet naval challenge. The Soviet fleet is first and foremost a submarine fleet. How does one fight a submarine navy with big carriers loaded with fighters and attack aircraft? Poorly, at best.

These changes will not be easy. Institutions will resist them strongly. At the very least, there will be genuine, and understandable, disagreement over how far the changes should go.

But no strategy lives forever. The world of 1983 is not the world of 1945. Pretending that nothing has changed in almost forty years would leave us burdened with obsolete responsibilities in some areas and dangerous weaknesses in others.

Military Reform

To support our military strategy, we must have effective tools. Fundamentally, this means effective conventional forces—forces that not only can deter war but also will prevail if challenged.

Today, our military effectiveness is in doubt. Vietnam, the *Mayaguez* affair, and the failed Iranian rescue attempt all suggest some deep-seated problems in our defense establishment.

Another look at the French example may help illuminate these problems. In pre-World War II Europe, France was considered the strongest military power, just as the United States is often considered the strongest in the world today. The French spent a great deal of money for defense, and they had the largest—and, by most contemporary accounts, finest—army in the world. They constructed the most massive fixed defense installation since the Great Wall of China—the Maginot Line.

But when World War II came, it all collapsed. In just over one month, France was utterly defeated.

What happened? Realizing that in combat ideas can be as important as weapons, the Germans had done some imaginative thinking and had revitalized and renewed their strategic and tactical doctrines after World War I. The French military, on the other hand, had become bogged down in paperwork and routine. Overall strategic and tactical thinking was abandoned as everyone protected his own little bureaucratic kingdom. As usual, where there was no vision, the people perished.

Unfortunately, my eight years on the Senate Armed Services Committee have convinced me that we are well along on the same road the French followed. Decades of spending more on a military that doesn't work have simply bought us a *bigger* military that doesn't work and, if anything, weakened our overall world military position. The time has come to identify and to fix what is wrong—not just buy more of it.

There are several specific areas where we need to ask new

questions and approach the defense debate differently. These areas require real reform—not just fine tuning.

PERSONNEL The first is manpower. It's the biggest slice of the defense budget and the element most important to victory. Wars are won by people, not by weapons. Yet our defense planning too often ignores the real needs of our troops and officers in the field.

Personnel questions are usually discussed in terms of pay, service entrance tests, and so on. Adequate pay is an absolute necessity for an effective military. But the debate over these matters overlooks many of the most critical issues in modern military personnel policy.

One such question is, what makes soldiers effective in combat? History tells us that, in war, soldiers don't fight for ideas or a paycheck—they fight for their buddies. If the person next to them is not a friend but a stranger, they are more apt to sit out the fight or break and run.

It takes time for strangers to come to trust one another. This trust, this cohesion, can develop only when the basic unit—the fire team, the squad, the aircraft crew, the ship's section—contains the same people over a long period of time. Today, we don't provide that time. Our troops are rotated from unit to unit at the highest rate in the world. Many Army combat companies have a personnel turnover rate of 25 percent every three months. So our troops remain strangers to one another, and strangers do not fight well together.

The current Army Chief of Staff, General Edward C. Meyer, has recognized this problem. Under his leadership, the Army is considering ways to improve unit cohesion, including adopting the British practice of having soldiers belong to a single regiment throughout their entire service career.

This initiative and others like it are vital if our Army is to be effective in combat. They are also important for the success of the all-volunteer force. Troops and noncommissioned officers are more likely to reenlist in a regiment where they can continue serving with their friends. The more people reenlist, the fewer new recruits we need.

There are internal factors that affect morale, but one major factor is external: the message communicated by ill-considered attempts to economize at the expense of our military personnel and their families. Such economy is false economy, for it strikes at the morale of our forces.

A military that feels unappreciated by the society it seeks to protect labors under a heavy burden. That is increasingly the case with our armed forces today. Over the past decade, there have been too many actions that have given servicemen and servicewomen the impression that their civilian leaders, including Congress, care little about them or their welfare.

We need to make it clear we *do* care. We need to assure our military personnel of a standard of living comparable to what they could expect as civilians. We need to provide adequate medical care and other benefits. And we need to ensure a secure retirement.

We do not want a mercenary military, a military where pay and benefits are the main motivations. But we cannot expect high morale in a force where many service personnel must choose between their service careers and the economic well-being of their families. We must provide adequate recompense for the risks and hardships inherent in military duty, and we must give solid assurance it will not be whittled away a few years hence.

OFFICER TRAINING AND PROMOTION The wrong questions are also asked in the training and education of our officers. Our military training system puts a premium on management skills, not military skills. We are producing officers more adept at boardroom strategy than battlefield strategy.

All organizations need a balance among several types of people—leaders, to motivate others to overcome obstacles; managers, to organize procedures and processes; and theorists, to determine what the product should be. In military service, the theorist's role is particularly important. It is the theorist, more than the leader or manager, who must understand war as a whole.

Unfortunately, in our armed forces today these three roles have gotten badly out of balance. Our military educational institutions too often stress management, not leadership or theory. As one West Point cadet recently wrote, "Cadets are not trained to think and lead, but rather to respond and manage, a situation that we [cadets] find deplorable."

Students at our defense colleges can pass through the entire curriculum without even hearing about issues such as military doctrine. A cadet can graduate from West Point or a midshipman from the Naval Academy with only a one-semester course in military history. Several years ago at the Marine Corps Command and Staff College, only about a dozen students signed up for the military history elective; several times that number took a course in aerobics and running. The Army Command and General Staff College at Fort Leavenworth recently expanded its physical education program; to make time for it, the military history reading requirement was reduced from ten books to only four.

A few of our military colleges have begun to teach about the nature, history, and theory of combat. The Naval War College reformed its curriculum several years ago to give greater attention to history. The Air Force Academy has just added four semesters of "military studies" to the one-semester history course. But these are the exceptions, not the rule.

Neither gym nor electrical engineering nor management courses are likely to help produce new George Pattons. Patton, himself a lifelong student of military history, once wrote to General Maxwell Taylor, then superintendent of West Point, "I am convinced that nothing I learned in electricity or hydraulics or in higher mathematics or in drawing in any way contributed to my military career. Therefore, I would markedly reduce or wholly jettison the above subjects."

Not only do we provide inadequate education in the military schools, we reinforce it with inadequate training in the field. To become an expert in tactics, a commander needs to spend time in the field in maneuvers that emphasize initiative and innovation.

He must face an opponent who is trying to surprise, confuse, and defeat him. Instead, many of our exercises follow rigid scripts, where everyone knows well in advance what he and his opponent will do and when. They stress management, not leadership or tactics. They resemble ballet more than war.

Then, through our promotion process, we ensure the manager's predominance by providing him with the surest rewards. Efficiency and "zero defects," the hallmarks of the successful manager, are currently the best tickets to career success. The leader and the theorist seldom meet the zero-defects test. Their imaginative approach to problems naturally leads to some mistakes, and the promotion system punishes them for these without rewarding them for innovation. So our problems persist and grow, while the underlying reasons for them go unrecognized and the proffered solutions remain conventional and uninspired.

Again, we need some changes in our fundamental policies. We need considerable revamping of the curricula of our military schools and colleges. They should emphasize warfare, not management; military history, not engineering—and above all they should teach *how* to think more than *what* to think. That is the real reason for studying military history. We do not need officers who can cite names and dates of battles, but officers who have learned how successful commanders thought their problems through and can use the same processes in conducting their own battles.

We also need to provide career rewards for those who become creative experts on combat. A first step would be to instruct promotion boards not to punish, but to promote those who seek new ideas, even though these people are sometimes difficult subordinates. Strong character, not compliant service to the system, should be the ticket to career success.

MILITARY DOCTRINE The third area requiring a new approach is military doctrine—the way our military would fight a war. Here, too, basics tend to be ignored. And, like the French in the 1930s, we are preparing to fight the last war.

Our Navy, for example, is really still designed to fight the carriers of the Imperial Japanese Navy. Yet the Soviet Navy relies primarily on submarines—which make our large carriers not only vulnerable, but also increasingly irrelevant.

Our approach to land warfare is similarly outdated. The American style of land war is still largely based on firepower and attrition, where the object is to destroy the enemy man by man, killing his troops and wrecking his equipment faster than he can do the same to us. We have fought this way for more than a century. The Union won the Civil War through firepower and attrition, overwhelming the Confederacy with more men and more guns, more supplies and more firepower. We rolled over the Central Powers in World War I and the Axis in World War II using the same approach.

But this style is badly outdated. Reliance on firepower and attrition can only work for the side with superior numbers, and we no longer have that advantage. We cannot assume we will be able to overwhelm the Soviet Union with superiority in manpower and matériel.

A different threat requires a different doctrine: maneuver warfare. Here the object is to destroy the enemy's ability to think clearly and act effectively in combat—by creating surprising and dangerous situations faster than he can cope with them. This is the way the British defeated the Argentines in the ground fighting for the Falkland Islands and it has been the guiding principle in most Israeli campaigns.

Because we cannot simply overpower the Soviets, we must learn to outsmart them. The world's greatest generals won by confusing and shattering their opponents—by breaking their will. We must learn to do the same.

During the past several years, a retired Air Force colonel named John Boyd has expanded the essence of maneuver warfare into a compelling general theory of conflict. Conflict, Boyd argues, is a matter of "observation-orientation-decision-action cycles," which each contending commander consistently repeats.

First the commander observes, not only with his eyes and ears but also with his radar, reconnaissance, and so forth. Then he orients—he forms a mental picture of his relationship to his opponent. On the basis of this picture, he determines a course of action—he decides. Finally, he acts. Then he begins observing again, to see the effect of his action.

The commander with the faster cycle will eventually win, because he is already doing something new and unexpected by the time the enemy gets to the action stage of his own cycle. The enemy's action comes too late to be effective. If one side is consistently faster, the enemy will fall further and further behind until he either panics or becomes passive. At that point, he has lost.

The Boyd theory is a tool of tremendous potential value. It offers us a way to outthink our opponents, instead of just spending vast sums to match their arms buildups. Massive arms stockpiles can be made obsolete not by duplicating them, but by anticipating their use and doing something unexpected just as they are put in service. We can put our enemies on a treadmill of perpetual obsolescence—in strategy, in tactics, and in equipment—if we plan along the lines of the Boyd concept.

The Army has taken some steps toward adopting the maneuver warfare idea and a doctrine based on the Boyd theory, and there is strong interest in parts of the Marine Corps. But even in these services the opposition is strong and the concepts are often misunderstood, while the Air Force and Navy remain uninterested or even hostile.

MILITARY EQUIPMENT Planning, of course, cannot be translated into action without adequate military equipment. That is the fourth area where military reform is needed.

Equipment tends to receive a good deal of public attention because we spend so much money on it. But even here, we miss the real issues and ask the wrong questions. Military equipment that we cannot afford in adequate quantities, or that simply does not work, will not give us effective fighting forces. And today, we are falling into both traps.

The Navy's big aircraft carriers provide the most obvious case of buying things that are so expensive we cannot afford them in the numbers we need. A single *Nimitz*-class aircraft-carrier task group—including planes and escort ships—costs about $17 billion. At that price, even the Reagan Administration's ambitious plans call for only fifteen carriers. So small a force could be decimated by the Soviet Navy's 290 attack submarines and 300 bombers, many of which are armed with modern anti-ship missiles.

In an era when each ship is increasingly vulnerable, we cannot afford to put all of our precious defense eggs in just fifteen vulnerable baskets—fifteen big carriers. We can better protect our naval aviation capability by dispersing it on a larger number of smaller ships.

Not only are we buying equipment so expensive we can't afford enough, we are buying equipment so complex it doesn't work well on the battlefield. Our weapons must work in combat—in rain and mud and heat and confusion. Only simple weapons are likely to do so. So we should concentrate on equipment that is affordable in large quantities and simpler to operate and maintain. And we need to keep the weapons we already have repaired, fueled, and ready. Spare parts for our equipment and fuel for our tanks aren't glamorous, but they are vitally important to our military success. *Readiness*—the stepchild of modern military planning—must be moved to the top of our security priorities.

Pentagon spokesmen have been calling military reform a debate between quality and quantity. They portray the services as supporters of quality, wanting only the finest weapons for our soldiers, sailors, and airmen. They argue that this necessarily leads to very costly, very complex weapons—the Army's new AH-64 attack helicopter, the F-18 fighter, the big nuclear aircraft carrier. In contrast, they say, the military reformers are willing to accept inferior weapons in order to buy more of them—or, sometimes, simply to save money.

In fact, the real debate centers on the meaning of quality. The Pentagon defines it only in technical terms: high technology equals high quality. The greater the technical advance, the better. We who urge military reform don't reject technological improvements, but we define quality tactically, according to the characteristics that are most important in actual combat.

These characteristics vary for each kind of weapon system, but in general they include:

- small size, because, in combat, being seen often means getting killed.
- simplicity, ruggedness, and ease of maintenance, because complex, fragile equipment is soon out of action and useless.
- rapid effect. Some highly touted antitank missiles, to cite one example, require that the gunner guide the missile for up to twenty seconds—and twenty seconds is a very long time to stand exposed when someone is shooting at you.
- finally, numbers, because in tactical terms quantity is also an aspect of quality. A navy that depends on only fifteen carriers is a vulnerable navy. The finest fighter plane in the world is in serious trouble if it is outnumbered three to one or five to one by enemy fighters.

Some of the characteristics that give a weapon tactical quality, such as small size and simplicity, also tend to make it cheaper. The practical choice today, therefore, is not between quality and quantity, but between technological complexity in small numbers of weapons and tactical quality in large numbers. To date, when confronted with that choice, the Pentagon has preferred the former. Reversing that trend must be a major objective of military reform.

OUR ARMED SERVICES AS BUREAUCRACIES Finally, we must examine how our military services function as institutions.

Traditionally, our armed forces were organized on a "corporative" or "socialized" model. Each officer was inculcated with, and worked in every way to advance, the overall goals and purposes of his service. Today, only the Marine Corps adheres to this model.

The Army, Navy, and Air Force have instead adopted a bureaucratic model, in which the officer specializes in one or several narrow functions, and the overall goals of the institution are supposedly attained by linking the "boxes" that define each individual's job. Unfortunately the narrow outlook this produces often causes those overall goals to be forgotten, while decisions are based on what all the little boxes within the institution find comfortable—which is to say, what they have done in the past.

Admiral Elmo R. Zumwalt, Jr., former Chief of Naval Operations, has described the way this mentality works in the Navy. The Navy has been divided into three competing branches or "unions" for the last quarter century—the aviators, the submariners, and the surface sailors. In his words, "Their rivalry has played a large part in the way the Navy has been directed. . . . Whichever union a commander comes from, it is hard for him not to favor fellow members, the men he has worked with most closely, when he constructs a staff or passes out choice assignments. It is hard for him not to think first of the needs of his branch, the needs he feels most deeply, when he works up a budget. It is hard for him not to stress the capability of his arm, for he has tested it himself, when he plans an action."

Bureaucratic behavior is our single most serious defense problem. It is a far more fundamental problem than any given year's budget level. War demands rapid change—presenting the enemy with the baffling and opaque, which resolves quickly into the threatening and dangerous. But change is bureaucratically uncomfortable. It upsets the existing arrangements, the traditional fiefs. In industry, bureaucratic behavior leads to bankruptcies. In government, it leads to massive waste. In war, it leads to defeat.

If we are to avoid the military dangers bureaucratization brings, we must reform the very basis of our armed services—the way they make decisions. Otherwise, all the other reforms will only be temporary, for the ongoing process of change and adaptation that must characterize an effective military will not develop. This may be the single most challenging defense task we face.

Early in this century, the British Navy underwent a series of dramatic and very controversial reforms at the hands of Admiral Sir John Fisher. In his 1923 book *The World Crisis, Part 1, 1911–14,* Winston Churchill wrote of these reforms:

> There is no doubt whatever that Fisher was right in nine-tenths of what he fought for. His great reforms sustained the power of the Royal Navy at the most critical period in its history. He gave the Navy the kind of shock which the British Army received at the time of the South African War. After a long period of serene and unchallenged complacency, the mutter of distant thunder could be heard. It was Fisher who hoisted the storm signals and beat all hands to quarters. He forced every department of the Naval Service to review its position and question its own existence. He shook them and beat them and cajoled them out of slumber into intense activity. But the Navy was not a pleasant place while this was going on.

The Pentagon may not be a pleasant place while we reexamine and reform our military services. But, as in Fisher's time, we can hear the distant thunder. It would be far less pleasant to confront the new realities for the first time on the battlefield.

The time for reform has come.

ACHIEVING
ENERGY SECURITY

———◆———

*The time to repair the roof is
when the sun is shining.*

—JOHN F. KENNEDY

Protecting our national security is not just a matter of reforming our military and curbing the nuclear arms race. We must also end our dependence on other countries—especially those in the volatile Middle East—for essential energy supplies. That dependence is as much a threat to the United States as an ineffective military or Soviet missiles. We learned in the 1970s that interruption of our supplies of foreign oil can cause personal hardship and economic disaster. But the risks of our dependence on imported oil are even greater. If we ever became engaged in a full-scale conventional war, much of our military strength would be diverted to the difficult task of safeguarding those supplies. Even worse is the possibility we could blunder into an unnecessary war in an unsuccessful effort to keep "our" oil flowing.

To have national security we must achieve *energy security*—the ability to withstand peacefully any foreign disruption of our energy supplies. Reaching this goal will take new government and business efforts to reduce our level of oil imports, to prepare to deal with their interruption, and to find more reliable ways of meeting our energy needs.

Some may think it alarmist to point out the possibility of the United States' going to war over oil. After all, the world oil market has been soft for over two years, with supplies exceeding demand. Our level of oil imports in 1982 was only half that of 1978. Prices have leveled off, even declined somewhat. Most Americans have forgotten the gas lines of the 1970s and now are worrying about other problems.

The energy "policy" of the Reagan Administration certainly does not suggest we are in any danger. The Administration has tried to cut our conservation and renewable-energy programs by 97 percent, to abandon any semblance of government preparation for supply emergencies, and to turn our remaining federal energy programs over to the Department of Commerce. The official justification for this effort to reverse energy efforts begun under both Democratic and Republican Administrations is to return energy to the "free market." But even this principle is undercut by the Administration's increased subsidies for nuclear power and leasing of federal energy lands at less than market value.

We are lucky this course has not yet led to disaster. The next major oil-supply disruption is only as far away as the next revolution in an oil-exporting nation or an expansion of the Iran-Iraq war. Our imports are down, but we remain vulnerable; we still are importing almost as much Middle Eastern oil as was cut off by the 1973 embargo, and more than was interrupted by the 1979 Iranian revolution. Clearly, the United States continues to be dangerously dependent on foreign oil.

These very real energy dangers, while overlooked by the Reagan Administration's *energy* policies, are revealed by its *military* policies. Secretary of Defense Caspar Weinberger has testified before Congress that the "umbilical cord of the West runs through the Strait of Hormuz into the [Persian] Gulf and the nations which surround it." To protect that umbilical cord, the Administration is spending tens of billions of dollars to expand the newly created Rapid Deployment Force, and millions more on new airfields and ports to let that force move into the Middle East's oil fields. Near the top of the Pentagon's list of priorities in the event of war, ranking behind only the defense of North America and of our NATO allies, is "ensuring access to the oil in Southwest Asia."

This preparation to send the United States to war for Persian Gulf oil is a disgrace to our national honor. We never should be reduced to shedding the blood of a single American in an unnecessary war for someone else's oil. As the world's most advanced nation, we can, and must, find peaceful and secure ways to meet our energy needs.

Going to war for oil would be not only a moral outrage, but also futile. Even a major military effort could not guarantee the continued flow of our oil imports. The region's oil wells, pipelines, and loading docks are all easy military targets, whether for terrorists, revolutionaries, or Soviet bombers. Oil tankers, lacking armor, defensive weapons, and maneuverability, and carrying inflammable cargo, would be easy prey for any military power—especially the Soviet Union, with the world's largest submarine fleet. In the end, going to war for oil would produce war, not oil. Only American coffins would flow back home.

Instead of relying on the Rapid Deployment Force to keep oil coming from the Middle East, we need an energy policy that will keep us from sending the RDF after oil. That policy should be designed to reduce our consumption of foreign oil to an acceptable level, low enough to prevent an interruption of oil imports from imperiling our economic security.

Achieving this energy security is necessary not only to eliminate the risk of sending American forces into the Middle East, but also to achieve sustained prosperity. Many of our economic problems are aggravated by our consumption of overpriced foreign oil. OPEC's fifteenfold increase of the price of oil during the 1970s was responsible for about one third of that decade's inflation. New supply disruptions would cause other surging increases in oil prices, creating both new inflation and a deeper recession.

Even without another oil supply disruption, we simply cannot afford to continue on our current course. In each of the first three years of the 1980s, we sent between $60 billion and $85 billion overseas to pay for foreign oil. This national monetary hemorrhage, unprecedented in the world's history, drains from our economy every year the equivalent of the combined net assets of General Motors, Ford, and IBM. We are paying for a bigger and better OPEC while the American economy stagnates.

Faced with the military and economic dangers of our dependence on foreign oil, only the most naïve leader would entrust our energy future solely to the private sector. OPEC is not operating a free market; it is manipulating the world oil market to its advantage. Protecting our national security is the job of the government, not the free market. Achieving energy security requires the commitment of our national government.

The government's role in achieving energy security has five parts:

- Building up our emergency stockpile of oil
- Reducing unnecessary energy consumption
- Developing new energy technologies
- Helping increase domestic energy production
- Authorizing a standby oil import fee

Protecting Against Disruption

Our most immediate need is to prepare for any oil supply disruption that occurs before we have reduced our imports of oil to acceptable levels.

A large stockpile of oil is the best defense against another oil cutoff. Yet eight years after Congress authorized the Strategic Petroleum Reserve, it holds only a third of its planned amount, barely enough to replace all imports for two months. Both recent Administrations are guilty of neglecting the reserve. The Carter Administration, although it called our energy problems the "moral equivalent of war," completely suspended filling the reserve to avoid angering OPEC. The Reagan Administration has made only halfhearted efforts to fill it.

We need to expand the reserve as rapidly as possible. It provides vital insurance against the consequences of being without oil, at a cost remarkably lower than that of many other national security expenditures. For the price of a single B-1 bomber, for example, we can buy enough oil to replace a week's imports from the Persian Gulf.

But just having an adequate oil reserve is not enough. We also need to plan now for the allocation of the stockpiled oil during an emergency. The Administration has not developed those plans, undercutting the effectiveness of any stockpile. If the government puts off planning for allocating the reserve until we are actually in an emergency, uncertainty will cause panicked competition for limited market supplies. The resulting increase in the price of crude oil could bring about many of the adverse effects of a supply disruption, especially hardship for those least able to afford new surges in the prices of home heating oil and gasoline. Advance government planning can avoid this unnecessary catastrophe, by instilling at the beginning of an emergency a general confidence that the government will maintain steady supplies.

The petroleum reserve is, of course, a short-term measure to limit the damage that could be caused by a supply disruption. The remaining elements of our energy policy should be designed to avoid those consequences altogether, by changing our energy habits so that we are no longer dependent on foreign oil.

Increasing Energy Efficiency

There are two ways to reduce our need for imported oil: increasing our production at home of oil and other energy supplies, and reducing our consumption of energy, especially oil. Although a balanced energy program must pursue both courses, there are several reasons why reducing consumption deserves the highest priority:

- Conservation is quicker. It takes only hours to insulate an attic, while it takes a new oil well eight years to reach peak production.
- Conservation is more lasting. Cutting back the amount of energy necessary to accomplish a task saves energy every time that task is performed. Continuing to use the same amount of energy increases the level of new supplies we must find every year, and accelerates the time when we will run out altogether.
- Conservation is more economical. The ways we use energy may have made sense ten years ago, when oil was $3 a barrel. But at today's energy prices there are so many cheaper ways to meet our needs that energy conservation probably is the most profitable investment available to the average American. Simply plugging the holes and cracks in the walls of our houses can save hundreds of dollars in home heating bills, as can tuning up the furnace annually.
- Conservation improves the quality of our life. Lower energy consumption does not require that we be "colder in the winter and hotter in the summer," as President Reagan once described it. Instead, if we focus on becoming more energy *efficient,* on getting more out of the energy we use, we can reduce our energy consumption without sacrifice. If we insulate our homes and tune up our furnaces, we can stay just as comfortable while using less energy –and consequently reducing the land disturbance and pollution that accompany the production and combustion of fossil fuels.

There are many reasons why energy conservation serves our interests, as individuals and as a nation, but the economic reasons are the most likely to lead to changes in our patterns of energy use. The government can limit its role to creating opportunities for market pressures to reduce today's high energy prices, by helping people find alternative ways of using energy. If energy users are given opportunities to adjust to the new economic reality—that it often is cheaper to save energy than to use it—their pocketbooks will dictate their choices without any need for government mandates. Only in a relatively few instances will government regulations, such as energy-efficiency standards, be necessary.

ENERGY INFORMATION Energy users' first need is information on the choices they have. We cannot become more energy efficient unless we know the relative costs of different ways of meeting our energy needs. Advocates of a free-market energy policy should remember that Adam Smith, the father of laissez faire economic policy, emphasized the importance of consumer information to the intelligent working of the marketplace.

Some of the necessary consumer information can be made available through existing educational systems. For example, the Brookhaven National Laboratory Energy Institute runs an energy course for high school science teachers. Since each teacher taking the course eventually comes into contact with hundreds or even thousands of future energy consumers, many people can be taught about today's energy realities at little federal expense. Such programs, now being curtailed by Administration budget cuts, should be expanded throughout the country.

The federal government can play another extremely important role simply by rating the relative energy efficiency of comparable goods, from tires to light bulbs. The success of the federal rating system for automobile fuel efficiency demonstrates how market pressures give manufacturers powerful incentives to make more efficient products.

The single most important new energy rating system would be one enabling home buyers to compare the energy costs of houses. Surveys conducted for realtors show energy costs have become the item of greatest concern to home buyers, overtaking such standard factors as the presence of a fireplace. But the difficulty of comparing home energy costs keeps this consumer preference from being a powerful market force.

With a standard measure to compare housing energy costs, home builders would be scrambling to make more energy-efficient houses, just as automobile manufacturers are working to make new cars more fuel efficient. The energy savings this would lead to are suggested by the "superinsulated" houses now being built. These homes retain enough of the occupants' body heat and heat from lights and appliances to eliminate the need for any heating system in all but the most severe climates. Yet the extra design and construction costs are low enough to be recovered through lower fuel bills in just two or three years.

FINANCIAL ASSISTANCE If information is a consumer's first need, financing often comes next. Information alone is enough to get people to invest in energy efficiency if the payback period is short, but many of us will not take advantage of improvements that take a year or more to pay for themselves.

Those without any spare money simply have no chance to invest in energy efficiency, even though they may have much to gain. To help these people we should expand such programs as low-income weatherization assistance, not eliminate them as the Reagan Administration has attempted. After all, these programs help us all. They help reduce our imports, hold down the expense of fuel-bill assistance programs, and—most important—give many of our citizens a chance to escape future energy payments that can condemn them to permanent poverty.

Most Americans, though, could afford some investments in energy efficiency, but simply do not want to make the immediate sacrifice of spending more now to reduce energy consumption later. To overcome this obstacle to our energy security, we need to turn long-term investments into immediate savings. For example, lenders could be required to consider future energy costs when they determine home buyers' eligibility for mortgages. This would recognize the economic reality that people can afford more expensive houses if their fuel bills are lower. For example, if the monthly fuel bill for a house is $100 below average, the home buyer can pay $100 more in each monthly mortgage payment—and buy a house perhaps $10,000 more expensive than he could otherwise afford. This would make energy-efficient housing available to more people, and would give builders and home-owners incentives to make their houses more efficient before putting them on the market.

ENERGY-EFFICIENCY STANDARDS In most cases, just making information and financial assistance available to energy users will be sufficient to bring about substantial reductions in energy use. But in some situations the personal motivation of potential savings is lacking. For example, owners of rental housing can pass along energy costs, and tenants may not stay in the same apartment long enough to make it worthwhile to improve its energy efficiency.

In cases like these, where normal market pressures are absent, mandatory energy-efficiency standards are needed. In particular, rental housing should be required to meet minimum thermal efficiency standards at the time of construction or resale.

This three-part program to improve energy efficiency—by providing energy information, financial assistance, and efficiency standards—can offer us valuable protection against oil supply disruptions. The less oil we use, the less we need to import, and the more time we have to find other reliable ways of meeting our energy needs in the future.

Developing New Energy Technologies

Sustained energy security will require major technological advances. Even if we become much more efficient in meeting our needs, we are just postponing the crisis unless we learn how to use new energy supplies and discover better methods of putting energy to use. We must also find ways to reduce the health and safety risks associated with some forms of energy use.

Fortunately, one of America's greatest assets is its unsurpassed technological ability. We need to apply that ability to our energy problems, to find new energy resources and new ways to use energy. We are more likely to outthink than to outproduce OPEC.

Federal leadership will be essential to make the technological breakthroughs we need. Private industry, which must account to shareholders for every penny that does not generate a profit, avoids research and development projects when the results are too uncertain, the benefits too diffuse, or the paybacks too distant. Also, some industries have virtually no capacity for research. The home construction industry, for example, is made up almost entirely of small companies with no spare capital to invest in developing more energy-efficient building designs. Finally, research usually is the first part of the budget to be cut during hard times. Private energy research initiatives have decreased substantially in the past two years because of the recession.

Simply put, if the federal government does not take the lead, we will not make the technological advances we need. Tragically, the Reagan Administration has tried to eliminate virtually all federal energy research programs. Even the programs identified by an early Administration task force as important have been slashed, from a modest $227 million in fiscal year 1981 to $18 million in FY 1983. And the private sector has not taken over this research, as the Administration hoped. A White House official concedes that "it is not clear that the industry sees the benefit of funding its own research and expanding its efforts to pick up the slack created by Federal withdrawal."

The government role in promoting new energy technologies can be twofold: traditional direct support of research and demonstration projects, and innovative use of government contracts to provide reliable markets for energy inventions.

We should not only restore the energy research funds cut by the Reagan Administration, but expand federal funding of energy research projects well beyond their historical levels. We should undertake more energy research at our national laboratories, expand the Solar Energy Research Institute, subsidize more research by universities and other private institutions, and establish new government-industry research centers patterned after the Health Effects Institute. That institute, jointly funded by the Environmental Protection Agency and automobile manufacturers, conducts research on the effects of automobile pollution on public health. The integrity of the research is guaranteed by an independent board of directors for the institute.

These federal efforts should be restricted to research and demonstration of first-generation technologies, leaving subsequent commercial activities to the private sector. The success of this pump-priming approach is evident in the results of some recent federal energy-research programs. For example, early federal studies on photovoltaic electricity overcame enough technological obstacles to encourage later private investment, and development of that technology has now brought us close to cost-effective ways of generating electricity from the sun.

Even more successful have been federal efforts to discover and demonstrate more energy-efficient ways to meet our lighting needs. Researchers at the Lawrence Berkeley Laboratory, one of our national laboratories, have discovered ways to improve fluorescent lighting to the point where it can be used in residential as well as commercial buildings. As a direct result of this research, the private sector is now beginning to market new light bulbs that require only one quarter as much electricity as conventional bulbs and cut lighting costs in half. Widespread use of this more efficient lighting could save us the equivalent of all the oil we now import from the Middle East.

In addition to funding research and development efforts directly, the federal government should make innovative use of its own need for energy supplies to provide a market for new technologies. Since the federal government is the largest energy user in the country, its purchases could substantially expand the market for new energy technologies.

Some tentative efforts in this direction are already being

made. For example, a new Veterans Administration hospital in Washington, D.C., will have an innovative air conditioning system that uses solar heat and chemical drying agents instead of electric motors to dehumidify air, potentially cutting energy consumption by 25 to 50 percent. Some of the savings will be used to monitor the performance of this new system. If it proves successful, we can not only save federal money by using the system in other new government buildings, but also document the savings for others seeking to reduce their cooling costs.

There are many other similar ways the federal government could stimulate energy innovation while meeting the government's own energy needs. For example, a few years ago Congress enacted a requirement that the Defense Department consider solar energy when designing new military facilities, and use solar systems whenever they would be cost effective. Under this legislation at least 265 different solar-energy systems are being installed on military bases, helping to create a growing market for renewable energy technologies.

These and similar federal efforts to accelerate the development of new energy technologies are just as vital to our future national security as weapons research, and should be given as high a priority.

Increasing Domestic Energy Production

Improving our energy efficiency is vital to reducing immediately our dependence on foreign oil, and promoting new energy technologies is vital to avoid continuing dependence in the future. But reliable supplies of conventional energy supplies will continue to be essential. We therefore need to produce more domestic energy—especially oil, natural gas, and coal.

Fortunately, the United States is blessed with an abundance of energy resources. Even though more oil and natural gas have been produced here than in any other country, our nation still ranks seventh in proved oil reserves and third in gas reserves.

Our actual oil and gas reserves may be far greater; there is mounting evidence we have staggering amounts of undiscovered natural gas. Our supplies of other fuels are even more abundant. The power of our rivers, the wind, and the sun is never ending. We have enough coal to sustain our current production rates for more than two centuries. Ninety percent of our fossil fuels is trapped in tar sands and oil shale, which we have not yet begun to tap.

With these abundant energy resources and the strength of our private energy industry, the government needs only to help create a climate in which the energy companies have a reasonable opportunity to make a profit. The most important step the government can take toward this is to bring about overall economic recovery, which would benefit energy industries as well as other parts of our economy. Two other, specific needs also require government action.

First, the windfall profits tax should be limited to just those wells now in operation. These wells are already profitable, even with the tax; if they were not profitable, they would not be in operation. But the current application of the tax to newly discovered oil should be terminated. It is an excise tax on the domestic petroleum industry, discouraging the additional production we need. Instead of discouraging the energy companies from competing with OPEC, we should give them a fair opportunity to outproduce and undersell the cartel.

The second specific need is for sound management of federal lands. The federal government owns one third of the nation's land area, and an even greater proportion of our energy-rich lands. Proper leasing of these lands for energy development is necessary to sustain adequate levels of production. That leasing must be the result of a careful process, not the Reagan Administration's automatic leasing of any lands that might contain energy resources. We need to restore the requirements for careful planning, consultation with state and local officials, and environmental protection that the Administration has jettisoned.

If the government, through these types of measures, provides the opportunity for private initiative by the energy industry, we will have enough domestic energy production to meet our needs.

Discouraging Oil Imports

If we follow the policies that have been outlined above, we should be able to reduce our oil imports to a safe level, and keep them at that level even as our population and our economy grow. But reducing imports is so crucial that we should authorize an oil import fee, to be imposed automatically if import levels increase or do not continue to decline. The fee should be linked to a schedule for additional, gradual decreases, reflecting the shifts away from foreign oil we should make if our programs are successful. Then, whenever imports rose above the scheduled amount, the fee would go into effect until imports again dropped to the planned level.

The import fee would strengthen the market forces that have led to reductions in imports over the past four years. Just as the high price of OPEC oil has encouraged additional investments in conservation and in domestic energy, the import fee would create an even stronger incentive to find other ways to meet our needs. The fee would supplement market pressures by including a national security premium in the price of foreign oil.

If the fee were ever imposed, revenues raised by it should be immediately rebated to individual energy users, to avoid causing personal hardship. The rebates should reflect regional differences in reliance on foreign oil, which would cause some parts of the country to pay more in fees. Thus those regions, such as New England, now relying most heavily on foreign oil would receive greater rebates, and those regions affected less would receive less.

Even if the import fee were never imposed, its mere existence as a standby measure would increase the effectiveness of the other elements of this national energy policy. It would provide certainty that new investments in conservation and alternative energy supplies could not be undercut by OPEC decisions to lower oil prices in new efforts to flood the American energy market.

Financing Energy Security

This five-part energy policy would achieve energy security. It also could be less expensive than our current policy. The new costs of this policy could be more than offset by reductions in the current enormous subsidies for nuclear power plants and commercial synthetic-fuel plants. These two types of projects receive the lion's share of federal energy expenditures, far more than can be justified by their relatively limited potential for solving our energy problems.

The greatest savings from reducing the subsidies for nuclear power would come from halting construction of the ill-conceived Clinch River nuclear breeder reactor. Its costs are now expected to rise to $8 billion, sixteen times the original projection. The need for the project has diminished even more rapidly than its costs have risen. The breeder is designed to produce more nuclear fuel than it uses to generate electricity, creating stable fuel supplies for other reactors. There may have been some merit to this idea when the nuclear industry was expanding rapidly and uranium was expected to become increasingly scarce and expensive. But nuclear power has not proved to be as economical as once expected, and utilities have not ordered a new nuclear power plant since 1978—indeed they've canceled thirty-eight planned reactors since 1980. Additional uranium discoveries and the halt to construction of new nuclear plants have combined to bring uranium prices down. As a result, even the supporters of Clinch River concede conditions will not make a breeder reactor commercially supportable until at least 2040.

An additional saving of as much as $15 billion could be achieved by abolishing the Synthetic Fuels Corporation. It is now clear that the SFC cannot overcome the economic and technological obstacles to immediate development of a full-scale commercial synfuels industry. Unable to lure private energy companies into synfuel investments even with its $15 billion in subsidies, the SFC now is considering building its own plants to meet its statutory synfuel production goals. A far sounder way to bring about advances in synfuels technologies would be to provide federal support in ways that do not involve such a major government intrusion into the energy marketplace, leaving with the private sector the major role in determining what forms of energy production warrant investments.

If we adopt energy programs such as these, we can replace our energy dependence with energy security. Drawing on a wider variety of domestic energy resources, and using them more efficiently, we can ensure the adequacy of our energy supplies for the future, stanch the flow of our dollars to oil-producing nations, and—most important—eliminate a grave threat to our economic and national security.

We can make this transformation, but we must begin now. So far, we have been lucky: the worst possible consequences of our energy dependence have not hit us. A prudent society will not count on continuation of that luck. Our security requires that we end the danger before the worst happens.

PREVENTING NUCLEAR HOLOCAUST

———◆———

*We have the power to
make this the best generation of
mankind in the history of the world—
or to make it the last.*

—JOHN F. KENNEDY

Every issue our nation faces, every goal we set for ourselves as a people, every dream we have for our children pales before the most important task of our time—the prevention of nuclear war.

For nearly forty years, nuclear weapons have posed the gravest threat to our security. Today, they are becoming an immediate threat to our survival.

For nearly forty years, nuclear weapons have had the power to render war unthinkable. Today, there are those who think about a limited nuclear war—and think it can be won.

For nearly forty years, our nation was determined to lead the world away from the abyss of nuclear war. Today, we have managed—incredibly—to abandon that sense of purpose.

Today, there are almost no constraints on the nuclear arms race between the superpowers, and new weapons are about to be deployed that could confound forever mankind's ability to put in place meaningful controls. The spread of nuclear weapons world-wide is unchecked. These developments are incompatible with the security of America; they are incompatible with the dream of America; and they are incompatible with the survival of America.

I can remember, as a high school student in Kansas, hearing early one morning a live radio broadcast of the rumbling of a nuclear test in the Nevada desert. These tests, and others in the Pacific Ocean, soon became everyday occurrences. Mushroom clouds from nuclear tests brought home to everyone the stark, awesome power of these weapons. However, since the signing in 1963 of the Limited Nuclear Test Ban Treaty, which prohibited nuclear tests aboveground, the nuclear explosions of the Soviet Union and the United States have been conducted out of sight, deep within the earth. Year by year, our appreciation of what these weapons could mean for our country and our civilization has become as detached from reality as old documentary films of doughboys in World War I, charging jerkily out of muddy trenches in the fields of France. Hiroshima is nearly forty years removed, and two generations have entered high school since the Second World War hinted to Americans of the tragedy and the desolation of total war.

Yet, as these memories have dimmed, the United States and the Soviet Union have increased immensely the nuclear destructive power at their disposal. From a few, relatively small nuclear weapons in our hands—and our hands *only,* in the late 1940s—the world's nuclear arsenals have grown to over 50,000 weapons possessing the destructive power of more than 5 billion tons of high explosives. Most of these warheads are not carried on slow-moving bombers that can be recalled; many will be flung on missiles with minutes for transit and moments for decision.

Nearly half of this vast assembly of nuclear explosive power is aimed—night and day—at targets in the Western world. Most of the remainder is aimed at similar targets in the Soviet bloc. Unleashed, these weapons would rip apart the fabric of our nations, destroy our societies, and reduce two once-proud countries to fifth-rate powers scrambling to keep life intact and, in the words of the statesman W. Averell Harriman, prey to any nation "caring to walk in our debris." The result of the past forty years is that we have, in the name of security, constructed a colossal edifice of insecurity for both our nations.

Were the enemy simply nuclear war, we could, in concert with the Soviet Union, dedicate ourselves with complete singlemindedness to its prevention. But these weapons and their stockpiles reflect the fear each superpower has of the other, and they have been assembled—on our part at least—to deter aggression by the Soviet Union.

As events have unfolded since World War II, the preparation of nuclear weapons to deter nuclear aggression has become the central nuclear strategy for both the United States and the Soviet Union. To put it simply, our nuclear weapons deter the Soviets from attacking us *by guaranteeing unacceptable damage in return.* Until we are able to eliminate all nuclear weapons from this planet, deterrence will remain our principal strategy for security and safety. Compromising deterrence through unilateral surrender or, conversely, discarding deterrence for insane visions of so-called limited nuclear war is a strategy for grave uncertainty at best and nuclear war at worst.

In seeking to prevent nuclear war we must work within the predictable construct of nuclear deterrence. But we must also prevent our good intentions from producing a world safer for conventional conflict.

The Challenge

Barely three years ago, it seemed as if we were indifferent as a nation to the nuclear threat. Today, we are witnessing an unprecedented outpouring of concern. This concern is articulate; it is genuine; it exists in every community in America; and it is increasingly well organized.

In November 1982, eight states and twenty-seven cities

across the United States voted for a nuclear freeze resolution, and many candidates supporting the freeze won election to Congress. The American people feel strongly about this issue—strongly enough to take the initiative to express their views directly.

American citizens understand—better than some of our leaders—that time is running out. They understand that if we do not restrain the arms race while we negotiate, we will be condemned, like Sisyphus, to endlessly push a great rock up a hill.

The freeze referenda that were adopted in 1982 were vitally important—they will force reluctant politicians to focus on the most important issue of our time. They were important because they sent President Reagan a signal to start taking the risk of nuclear war seriously.

When President Reagan was elected in 1980, few in this country anticipated such a citizen movement. The very idea of seeking to control arms had been under systematic attack—politically and ideologically—for several years, and the election of the new President appeared to vindicate this attack. The chances for American ratification of the SALT (Strategic Arms Limitation Talks) II nuclear weapons treaty were declared to be nil. And America's Chief Executive seemed ready to remove the control of arms from our national agenda. Indeed, after several months in office, President Reagan could announce (and hear almost no word of criticism), "The argument, if there is any, will be over which weapons [we buy] and not whether we should forsake weapons for treaties and agreements."

In the period that has followed, we have seen inaction in the face of the most profound threat to our security. We have seen attempts to dismantle the progress achieved by six Presidents to make ours a safer world. And we have heard a steady procession of irresponsible statements about nuclear war that have alarmed friend and foe alike.

I don't know whether this Administration's massive nuclear buildup and irresponsible statements frighten the Russians, but they certainly frighten a lot of Americans. A nation whose children go to bed at night with nuclear nightmares is not a secure nation.

We must build on this citizen movement to develop a comprehensive arms control agenda that will not only freeze the number of nuclear weapons but reduce the likelihood they will ever be used. Nineteen eighty-three is the year to make progress on arms control. If we haven't made *substantial* progress before 1984, we'll be caught up in the 1984 elections. And both the United States and the Soviet Union will then stop to see what will happen that November.

Concern about the dangers of nuclear war, however, will not be sufficient to achieve progress. Faced with the growing threat of nuclear weapons, it will take a supreme effort of national and international will to reduce the risk of nuclear conflict and carry us safely into the twenty-first century. We must engage our nation in what can only be called the noblest expression of the idea of America—leadership for peace with security.

If we are to make this supreme effort, if we truly are to engage our nation, we must first banish five pervasive myths.

The first myth is that seeking to control nuclear weapons amounts to being soft on security. Verifiable arms limitations, if they reduce the threat of nuclear war, enhance our national security. They are checks on our adversaries, not rewards to our friends. And to the precise extent that arms control agreements limit the size of the Soviet nuclear force, they are *essential* to our security. It is outrageous that certain opponents of arms control are allowed to pose as patriots, when their success in opposing and obstructing verifiable limits has resulted in more Soviet weapons targeted on more American cities and towns. They have cheapened the meaning of peace through strength and have been permitted to turn upside down the definition of security in the nuclear age.

In cold, practical military terms, we are more secure if we know what nuclear forces the Soviets have, where they are deployed, and how many will be deployed five years from now.

We can achieve this only through carefully drawn, verifiable limits on arms. We are more secure if we can keep as low as possible the number of nuclear warheads on each Soviet missile. We are more secure if the Soviets are not allowed to conceal deployments of their missiles or interfere with our ability to observe their forces. We are more secure if there are fewer nations that can launch a nuclear weapon against our soil. We are more secure if our defense resources are devoted to meeting the more likely military threat—conventional conflict—not squandered on an endless, avoidable nuclear arms race.

The second myth is that negotiated arms control means trusting the Russians. Anyone who has participated in any arms negotiations with the Soviet Union knows that trust is nonexistent in these meetings. Every provision we negotiate is judged by our own *independent* ability to ensure the Soviets are living up to what they have signed. Our military and intelligence leaders have been involved every step of the way, from establishing our negotiating position to actual negotiations with their Soviet counterparts. Indeed, in recent years, the most steadfast supporters of continued arms negotiations have been our own Joint Chiefs of Staff. We have, as well, spent tens of billions of dollars assembling the most sophisticated intelligence systems in the world to monitor Soviet forces, particularly those subject to arms agreements. With these systems, we are able to know, for example, when a Soviet SS-19 intercontinental ballistic missile is deployed, where it is deployed, the power of its engines, and how many nuclear warheads it can carry.

The third myth is that unilateral disarmament holds our best hope for averting nuclear war. Such a course could lead to the war we must prevent. It would encourage dangerous miscalculations by adversaries we intend to deter. The profound paradox of our time still stands—the very terror of these weapons prevents their use.

The fourth myth is that the spread of nuclear weapons around the world is an issue separate and distinct from the superpower arms race. In fact, the two are intimately related. It is sheer arrogance to believe that the United States and the Soviet Union can increase their nuclear forces beyond any rational level and still expect other nations to forgo these weapons.

No longer are there two or three nations that possess the power of ultimate destruction; now there are six. In a decade, there could be ten or twenty or more. Can anyone say with confidence that Iraq or Libya will show restraint in the use of nuclear weapons? And what of the terrorist groups now active in many nations? For these groups, the building blocks to achieving nuclear status are not armies of scientists working on expensive, hard-to-assemble, complex technologies. They are a few individuals building a crude nuclear device with basic physics and a few pounds of plutonium. It is, therefore, dangerously naïve to believe we can promote the spread of nuclear materials around the globe and not one day see the Fifth Horseman of nuclear terrorism ride down upon some American, European, or Israeli city.

The final myth is that we can afford to wait, that nuclear war simply will not happen, that other problems come first. No myth is less worthy of belief or more dangerous. Today arms cannot be piled on arms without consequence—not on a globe where once-distant enemies are today's neighbors, where the weapons we have today will be the weapons of others tomorrow.

Regrettably, there is no magic formula to end the arms race and prevent the use of nuclear weapons. It has become fashionable to blame the "failures" of arms control on our inability to muster broad-based popular support for sensible limits on weapons. It is even more fashionable to blame "experts" for making the subject too complex. These are delusions. What we plan to do can and must be explained in clear, straightforward terms, and it must enlist our imagination and hope. What we actually do *will* be extraordinarily complex and difficult, for we are dealing with decades of mutual suspicion. We are dealing as well with the technological prowess of each superpower in producing weapons ever more fiendish in their ability to defy our technical and political ability to control them. And we are dealing with the gruesome desire of many countries to assert their national pride with deadly weapons. There are, however, common sense steps to be taken—steps that can, with will, put us on a course toward peace and security.

Prevention: A New Focus

We must direct our nation's military policies toward prevention of the use of nuclear weapons. This must be the central organizing principle in arms negotiations and in the programs we undertake to remain militarily strong.

Prevention of the use of nuclear weapons will require restraint in arms, but it requires provision of arms as well, for we must maintain a convincing, invulnerable nuclear deterrent so no nation, under any circumstances, could ever believe that it might find profit through nuclear attack. This will require selective modernization of our strategic nuclear forces, particularly those based on missile submarines at sea, which are invulnerable now and will remain so for decades to come. Our nuclear forces must be reliable; they must be survivable; we must be able to communicate effectively with them; and any potential aggressor must know that—if called upon—these weapons can penetrate to their targets.

In this connection, it is vital for nuclear deterrence that we improve our nuclear force control and communications to make it impossible for the Soviet Union to disarm or disable our command structure with a few well-directed nuclear weapons. This aspect of our deterrent has been underemphasized in the past, despite its key importance in our retaliatory capability. But prevention goes beyond maintaining a strong nuclear deterrent, for confusion, fear, and ignorance could bring on the war we seek to avoid, just as surely as weakness or lack of resolution.

It follows that we must devise new measures to prevent the possibility of a nuclear exchange through accident or miscalculation. In 1980, Senator Barry Goldwater and I conducted a Senate Armed Services Committee investigation into the continuing serious problems with our strategic warning system. We discovered that during an eighteen-month period this warning system registered 151 false alarms—one of which lasted a full six minutes, or half the time it would take a submarine-launched ballistic missile to reach its target in the United States.

We can only speculate as to how reliable Soviet personnel and computers are, but there is no reason to suspect that the Soviets are immune to these problems. We should establish a joint Soviet-American crisis control facility in which senior civilian and military personnel from both countries would monitor nuclear-weapons-related activities, including test launches of missiles. This facility could also prove useful in preventing a wider war should a nuclear terrorist ever threaten either of our countries. In addition to this new facility, we should update the 1963 hotline agreement to ensure instant, continuous, and secure communications between the United States and the Soviet Union in a crisis.

Prevention of nuclear war also requires improved intelligence collection. The most valuable satellites our nation has are those that watch night and day for signs of a Soviet attack. There is no margin for error. Other satellites follow the deployment of Soviet forces and thus enable us to plan our military strategy based on information, not fear or speculation. These satellites help us verify that the Soviets are complying with the arms limitations agreements they sign. Indeed, it would probably be impossible to have any arms limitation agreements at all without these and other technical observation capabilities. They are systems upon which hawk and dove can and should agree, and we must relentlessly pursue any avenue we can to improve and protect them.

Nuclear war could also begin if one nation in a crisis believed its nuclear forces—or even a portion of them—could be destroyed, and therefore struck first, preferring to "use it rather than lose it." Highly accurate, multiple-warhead land-based missiles are beginning to present this danger, providing strong incentives to strike first. For this reason, new weapons, no matter how attractive they look, must be judged by the standard of whether they will increase or decrease the risk of nuclear war. The Soviet SS-18 heavy missile is one such threatening weapon; our proposed new MX missile is another.

This highly accurate missile—wherever it is based—will be a tempting target for the Soviets, because they know each MX will be able to knock out five to ten Soviet missiles at a time. That could encourage the Soviets to try striking first. With this in mind, these most destabilizing weapons should be prime candidates for elimination in any arms negotiations.

Since 1976, more than thirty proposals for basing the MX have been thoroughly examined by two Administrations. All have been discarded for a variety of technical, political, and environmental reasons. No plan has yet been devised which, if implemented, would ensure the long-term survivability of the American missile force.

The plan proposed in 1982—the ill-named Dense Pack—is no more promising and in many ways worse than its predecessors. It would cost up to $25 billion for only a few years of protection. We then would be required to violate the most successful arms control treaty ever concluded—the anti–ballistic missile treaty of 1972—by building antimissile weapons to protect the MX.

Rather than commit this country to an ill-considered and unworkable plan for basing the MX on land, we should begin active consideration of other ways to guarantee the effectiveness of our strategic forces. The first and most important way to reduce the likelihood of nuclear war is to redouble our efforts to negotiate an equitable, comprehensive, and verifiable nuclear arms control agreement with the Soviet Union. Another way is to reduce the importance of land-based missiles in our strategic nuclear posture by shifting many of our nuclear weapons to other delivery systems, such as ballistic-missile submarines and standoff bombers equipped with cruise missiles.

Finally, prevention of nuclear war requires maintenance and strengthening of our conventional armed forces so that nuclear weapons are our last line of defense, not our only means of response. One of the most likely paths to a nuclear conflict would be nuclear escalation because we were too weak to turn back a conventional enemy attack with our nonnuclear forces.

All of these measures should demonstrate that the prevention of nuclear war is not one policy or one course of action. It is a combination of actions with one common objective. Some actions, such as some of those I have already mentioned, we could carry out independent of other countries. Other courses we must pursue to prevent the use of nuclear weapons will require negotiations with our principal adversary, the Soviet Union. And it is to these that we must turn.

Laying the Foundation

In negotiations with the Soviet Union, it is essential that we attend to old business even as we move on to a new arms control agenda.

The most important task in this regard is Senate ratification of the SALT II treaty, which limits strategic nuclear arms. Signed in 1979 after seven years of negotiations by three American Presidents, two of them Republican, the SALT II treaty has not been ratified, and it was opposed by President Reagan both before and after his election. Yet, the treaty still exists. It is still before the Senate, and neither nation has done anything inconsistent with the provisions of the treaty.

Until ratified, this treaty does not have the full force of law, nor can we expect it to last forever through the ups and downs of Soviet-American relations. Leaders in both countries will be tempted to deploy new weapons that could forever render the treaty meaningless. It is time to ratify SALT II. We are already abiding by most of its terms, and I, like former Secretary of State Henry Kissinger, "have great difficulty understanding why it is safe to adhere to a non-ratified agreement, while it is unsafe formally to ratify what one is already observing."

SALT II would reduce the dangers of the arms race and enhance our security in a number of concrete ways:

- It would require the Soviet Union to dismantle more than 250 bombers and missiles, or more than 10 percent of its entire strategic nuclear forces.
- It would prevent Soviet deployment of additional nuclear weapons systems, such as new intercontinental ballistic missile launchers, or more than one new type of land-based intercontinental ballistic missile (they have several under construction now), or more than ten nuclear warheads on their SS-18 heavy missile (each of which could actually carry thirty warheads or more).
- It would continue regular Soviet-American exchanges of information on important nuclear weapons issues, such as the flight testing of missiles.
- It would prohibit the Soviets from deliberately concealing their strategic nuclear forces from our observation satellites, or interfering with our ability to count their forces.

These advantages and others make it imperative that we and the Soviets ratify SALT II as soon as possible. In the absence of ratification, the Reagan Administration at a minimum should do what it has long delayed: issue an unambiguous declaration of its intent to abide by the terms of SALT II and its predecessor, SALT I, as long as the Soviet Union abides by them as well. We should also seek a similar declaration from the Soviets.

Such a declaration would do more than clear the air. It would reestablish the consistency of United States policy in an area where the steadiness of our purpose has become suspect to many. The anxiety that has fed discord at home over our commitment to peace has been mirrored and intensified and exploited to divide us from our allies around the world. Instead of strengthening our hand, Reagan Administration policy has weakened Western cohesion. It is past time to correct our course.

Linked with ratification of SALT II should be a series of companion actions. The first would be a strong reaffirmation of the 1972 anti-ballistic missile treaty, which has prevented an arms race in highly expensive and almost certainly unworkable defensive missile systems.

The reasons for which we signed this treaty are as valid today as they were ten years ago. Yet, Reagan Administration officials have repeatedly indicated that if they can design an anti-ballistic missile system that they *believe* will work, then the ABM treaty will be modified or discarded. What a sad day it would be for America if we were to discard a solemn treaty, not because such an action was vital for our security, but simply because it was believed to be convenient to do so!

A second measure would be to resume negotiations with the Soviet Union to ban entirely—or at least restrict if a complete ban cannot be achieved—the testing and deployment of antisatellite weapons. Both our nations are fast developing weapons that could disrupt command, control, communications, and intelligence capabilities, vital to preventing a nuclear crisis from escalating to nuclear war and to limiting the use of nuclear weapons if conflict should ever occur. It is also in our particular military interest to prevent a full-fledged arms race in space, for we, more than the Soviets, are dependent on communications and intelligence systems based in space.

Other companion measures would be resumption of negotiations for a ban on all nuclear testing for all time, and ratification of the 1974 threshold test ban treaty (which limited underground nuclear explosions to 150 kilotons) and its 1976 companion, the peaceful nuclear explosions treaty, which contains unprecedented Soviet concessions regarding on-site inspection. These two treaties, signed more than six years ago, still have not been ratified by the Senate.

These measures—from ratification of SALT II to resumption of negotiations for a complete nuclear test ban—will restore continuity in the control of arms. They are vital steps, but they are only a prelude. For even if we were to take them all, we would have only regained lost ground. We must do more than regain lost ground, for time is certainly not now on our side.

A New Arms Control Agenda

Time is why we must develop a new arms control negotiating agenda. This agenda must be comprehensive; it must be pursued with urgency; and it must be far-reaching. It is not enough to focus only on this year or the next, for many of the weapons built today will be part of our arsenals three decades from now.

In February 1982, I introduced a Senate resolution making the focus of new strategic negotiations the prevention of the use of nuclear weapons. Like the nuclear freeze, such a focus would include reductions in the size of our arsenals, but it would also require the negotiation of measures to (1) prevent the use of nuclear weapons through accident or miscalculation; (2) eliminate the most destabilizing weapons; and (3) prevent the further spread of nuclear weapons to countries not now possessing them.

Nuclear arms reductions should eventually aim to cut the superpowers' nuclear weapons arsenals by 50 percent, as advocated by Americans as diverse as our former ambassador to the Soviet Union, George Kennan, and our former Commander in Chief in the Pacific, Admiral Noel Gayler. We should be under no illusions. This outcome will be difficult to achieve, for we are

attempting to reduce two enormous, hostile military machines—the products of different technological styles, different
geographies, different political beliefs, and different military requirements. The result of our effort should not simply be numeri-
cal reductions for, if they were designed improperly, we could
emerge even less safe than we are today. We must establish a
stable Soviet-American military relationship wherein neither pro-
tagonist has any incentive to start a nuclear war.

   Therefore, the immediate goal in negotiations with the Soviet
Union should be to reduce and eventually eliminate highly accurate multiwarhead (MIRVed) land-based missiles, which pose a
formidable threat to parts of the retaliatory forces of each side. A
number of plans have been advanced to realize this objective. I
believe the most promising negotiating course is to designate sin-
gle-warhead missiles as the only land-based missiles permitted on
either side.

   For the past five years or more, Americans have heard about
the vulnerability of our land-based missiles. This vulnerability has
arisen because the development of multiple-warhead technologies, coupled with improvements in missile guidance systems, has
now made it possible, at least in theory, for one missile to eliminate between three and ten missiles of an adversary. This, as
noted earlier, could put a premium on striking first.

   The key to reducing the vulnerability of land-based missiles
lies in reducing their value as targets. Allowing only missiles with
a single warhead would accomplish this in two ways simultaneously. First, the attacker would be unlikely to strike first, because
he would have to expend more warheads in the attack than he
could hope to destroy. And second, the total number of land-
based missile warheads would decline, both absolutely and as a
proportion of the total in each nation's nuclear force. As a result,
we would reinforce the importance of survivable nuclear weapons systems—bombers and missile-carrying submarines—which
are less likely to provoke a nuclear attack.

The New Threat: Nuclear Terrorism

We could achieve every objective listed so far and still the business of preventing nuclear war would be only half-done, for today we face an additional grave danger—*the spread of nuclear weapons.*

Today, six countries—the United States, the Soviet Union, Great Britain, France, China, and India—have built and tested nuclear weapons. Several other nations, such as Pakistan, Argentina, South Africa, and Israel, have shown a keen interest in joining the "nuclear club." As many as twenty nations may have nuclear weapons by the end of the decade.

In addition, there are more than 800 nuclear facilities dedicated to the production of nuclear power and research. Through diversion of nuclear materials from civilian use, many of these facilities could become the building blocks for nuclear weapons programs, and this risk is certain to increase if the use of plutonium—the most dangerous nuclear material—becomes widespread.

The prospect that additional countries, particularly those with less stable regimes, could obtain nuclear weapons is terrifying. As more countries come to possess nuclear weapons, the "balance of terror" that so far has restrained the superpowers from nuclear conflict will have increasingly less deterrent effect.

The consequences of the spread of nuclear weapons are alarming:

- As each new country joins the nuclear club, the risk of a regional nuclear arms race, and possibly regional nuclear war, increases. Such an arms race began in 1974 after India tested a nuclear bomb. If a regional nuclear war broke out between India and Pakistan, between Israel and an Arab country, or elsewhere, each superpower may become involved to protect its ally, thus perhaps turning the regional conflict into global conflagration.

- A fanatical leader could acquire a nuclear weapon and feel no compunctions about using it. What if Iran had already received the nuclear material and equipment the United States had promised to sell it when the Ayatollah Khomeini came to power?

- Finally, nuclear weapons could become the ultimate tool of terrorists. Terrorists already have access to the information needed to build a crude nuclear bomb—in technical journals, encyclopedias, and other public literature. Undergraduate students at Princeton University and the Massachusetts Institute of Technology and postgraduate students at the Atomic Energy Commission have used unclassified information to produce bomb designs that experts determined would work.

A crude nuclear bomb would have one thousandth the explosive power of a modern hydrogen bomb. But that is still the yield of the atomic bomb dropped on Hiroshima. And if exploded on Wall Street during office hours, it would kill as many as 1 million people. Elsewhere in New York, or in another large city, it would kill from 50,000 to 100,000 people.

To prevent the spread of nuclear weapons, we must persuade new countries to sign the nuclear nonproliferation treaty, through which 113 nations have already forsworn nuclear weapons. With our companion superpower, the Soviet Union, we will have to set an example by restraining our own nuclear weapons program. But most of all, we must be willing to eliminate the international trade in nuclear materials and technology.

For three decades, we have tried to maintain a distinction between peaceful and military uses of nuclear energy. But the fact is, no such distinction exists. A country can say it wants sensitive nuclear technology and material solely for its civilian nuclear power program, while really planning to use it to build a bomb.

To date, nuclear reactors around the world have produced about 140 tons of plutonium—enough to build more than 20,000 Nagasaki-sized bombs. So far, most of that plutonium remains locked in spent reactor fuel. But a technology known as reprocessing can extract the plutonium, so it can be used again to fuel nuclear reactors—and to build weapons. Several countries, including France and Great Britain, have begun to reprocess spent fuel as a commercial venture and even to build breeder reactors. Other countries have shown increasing interest in acquiring these technologies. If the trend continues, we could enter a Plutonium Economy where every year thousands of tons of weapons-usable or "separated" plutonium would move in international commerce, susceptible to theft or diversion.

In the face of this proliferating threat to our security, the Reagan Administration has made no attempt to control it, and has in fact *promoted* the spread of American nuclear materials and technology around the world. It has lifted a ban imposed by President Ford on reprocessing. It has waived restrictions on aid to Pakistan despite that nation's clandestine nuclear weapons development program. It has agreed to sell nuclear fuel to Brazil—a nation that has not signed the nuclear nonproliferation treaty forswearing the acquisition of nuclear weapons. The Administration has sold computer technology destined for a hush-hush nuclear facility in Argentina and it has allowed India to circumvent American law in buying fuel.

Finally, at home, the Administration has considered reprocessing spent commercial nuclear fuel to create additional plutonium for military purposes, and is actively promoting the multibillion-dollar and already technically obsolete Clinch River breeder reactor.

With these policies, we are cutting short the brief time left to prevent the future spread of nuclear arms.

At a minimum, we and the other nuclear suppliers must recognize that the world's interest in peace, security, and survival far outweighs the economic benefits of nuclear trade. We should make separated plutonium as difficult to obtain, and as uneconomical to use, as possible. *This will require an immediate international plutonium freeze.*

First, we must halt the further production of separated plutonium—for both military and civilian purposes. Such a freeze should not be unilateral; rather, the United States, the Soviet Union, and other plutonium-producing nations should enter into a multilateral agreement to halt their plutonium production. This agreement could be verified with inspections by the International Atomic Energy Agency, the body responsible for administering the safeguards currently applied to many civilian nuclear activities worldwide.

By freezing the world plutonium inventory at current levels, this agreement would limit the availability of separated plutonium and thus the risk that a country or terrorist group could obtain enough, through theft or diversion, to build nuclear weapons. Yet a plutonium freeze would do more than make it difficult for non-nuclear weapons states and terrorists to join the nuclear club. It would also affect the arms race between the superpowers by setting outside bounds to it—the amount of separated plutonium remaining in the international stockpile.

Second, nuclear supplier nations must agree not to export the technology to produce plutonium, such as spent-fuel reprocessing and breeder reactors. Halting the export of this technology will substantially reduce the risk that nations such as Libya will circumvent an international freeze on plutonium production.

Finally, all the nations of the world—nuclear suppliers and consumers alike—should supplement the first two agreements by rejecting the commercial use of separated plutonium as a nuclear power reactor fuel. In return, supplier nations should make available abundant and secure supplies of natural and low-enriched uranium fuel, materials not directly usable for weapons.

Rejecting the commercial use of plutonium will mean, at

home, terminating construction of the Clinch River breeder reactor. Breeder reactors not only encourage the global spread of plutonium, but are also economically unjustifiable.

Preventing the use of nuclear weapons, reducing nuclear arms, stopping the spread of plutonium—these are commonsense steps toward a more secure America and toward a future for our children and their children's children.

More than twenty-five years ago, in November 1957, General Omar Bradley told a school convocation, "If I am sometimes discouraged, it is not by the magnitude of the problem, but by our colossal indifference to it. I am unable to understand why—if we are willing to trust in reason as a restraint on the use of a ready-made ready-to-fire bomb—we do not make greater, more diligent and more imaginative use of reason and human intelligence in seeking an accord and compromise which will make it possible for mankind to control the atom and banish it as an instrument of war."

Today we have begun to alter this "colossal indifference," and with this beginning we have moved toward a safer world. For if we are forced to think about nuclear war—to contemplate its likelihood and its consequences—then we, our families, our communities, and our nation will be compelled to act.

Individually, we each have our vision, our own ideal of what we want this country to stand for and accomplish. But I believe these personal visions share at least one idea in common—that the purpose of America is peace, a secure peace.

Without this purpose, we will fail. With this purpose, a generation can fashion its place in history. In such purpose, there is hope.

CONCLUSION

———◆———

*It is not yesterday, tradition, the past which is
the decisive, the determining force in a nation. Nations are made,
and go on living, by having a program for the future.*

—José Ortega y Gasset

This book is, in one sense, the last step on a long road. It is the culmination of years of discussion and thinking and work with many people whose thoughts and views are included here. But in many other ways, this modest effort is just the beginning. No ideas, however sound or exciting, can work unless they win the test of public discussion and debate. I've tried, in this book, to set the terms of the debate in several major public policy areas of the future. I've had my chance to put forward some of my views. Now I hope others, inside government and outside, will respond to the challenge and carry on the public debate our country deserves.

I am embarking on a campaign for the nomination of my party to be President of the United States. I hope to win. But more importantly, I hope to be prepared to govern. To me, that requires a willingness to put forward specific proposals, to test ideas, and to seek others' views and guidance during this crucial campaign process. I don't expect all the other candidates to take this route. It is potentially risky to provide so many specifics that others can criticize. But 1984 must be a year in which our people truly debate the kind of future they seek, and how they intend to achieve it. And I hope this book will contribute to that debate.

It contains elements of my vision for an America that my children can be proud of.

INDEX

Agricultural exports, 75–76
Agriculture, 51
American Defense Education
    Act, 91–92
Anti-ballistic missile (ABM)
    treaty, 169
Antisatellite weapons, 169
Armed forces, *See* Military,
    the

Basic Educational
    Opportunity Grants
    program, 94
Boyd, Col. John, 135–36
Bradley, Bill, 42
Bradley, Gen. Omar, 176
Bridges, 35
Buchan, John, 8
Budget(s), 33
    for capital investment, 34–
    36
    defense, 31–32, 123
    priorities for, 30–33
    Reagan Administration, 28,
    30–31
Budget deficits, 28, 30–33
Bureaucracy, military, 138–
    40

California Economic
    Adjustment Team
    (CEAT), 98–99
Capital, venture, 54–59
Capital investment, budget
    for, 34–36
Choate, Pat, 102
Churchill, Winston, 140
Clinch River nuclear breeder
    reactor, 155, 174, 176

Colleges and universities,
    86–88
Connecticut Product
    Development Corporation
    (CPDC), 57
Control Data Corporation,
    104–5, 114–15
Corporate taxes, 40
Council on Emerging Issues,
    proposal for, 80–81

Defense, 123–40
    strategy for, 126–29, 143
    See also Nuclear war,
    prevention of
Defense budget (military
    spending), 31–32, 123
Deficits, budget, 28, 30–33
De Gaulle, Charles, 125
Developing nations, exports
    to, 74
Dirksen, Everett, 49
Displaced workers,
    employment of, 98–100,
    103

Economic growth, 33
Economy, the:
    international. *See*
    International economy
    key areas for action in, 25–
    26
    structural changes in, 20–21
    See also Budget(s);
    Employment; Industry;
    Tax(es); Trade
Education:
    American Defense
    Education Act and, 91–92
    continuing, 115–16

employment and, 86–88,
    90–93
    military, 133, 134
Elderly, the, in the labor
    force, 23–24
Employee stock ownership
    plans (ESOPs), 113–14
Employment, 83–117
    of displaced workers, 98–
    100, 103
    education and, 86–88, 90–
    93
    fields that will generate
    new, 85–86
    labor force growth and, 85
    training and retraining
    workers, 88–96, 100–107
    See also Work
Energy, 12, 15
    foreign sources of, 122–23
Energy conservation, 146–47
Energy efficiency, 145–49
Energy-efficiency standards,
    149
Energy information for
    consumers, 147–48
Energy security:
    discouraging oil imports
    and, 154–55
    energy efficiency and, 145–
    49
    financing, 155–56
    increasing domestic energy
    production and, 152–54
    protecting against oil supply
    disruption and, 144–45
    technological advances and,
    149–52
Enlightenment programs, 32
Entrepreneurs, reforms to
    encourage, 54–59

Equality, 10–11
European Community, 75
Export financing, 72–73
Export-Import Bank, 73
Exports:
  promotion of, 72–77
  See also Trade

Fair tax, 42–44
Federal Reserve Board, 29–30
Financial institutions, easing regulations on, 55–57
Fiscal policies, 27–29
  See also Budget; Tax(es)
Fisher, Sir John, 140
Flat tax, 41–42
Flexible hours (flextime), 114–15
Ford, Henry, 49
Ford Motor Company, 107
Foreign Commercial Service, 73–74
France, 128; 130

General Agreement on Tariffs and Trade (GATT), 68, 69, 75–78
Gephardt, Richard, 42
Government regulations, on private financial institutions, 55–57

Hall, Robert, 42
Hansen, Derek, 56
Hawaii Entrepreneurship Training and Development Institution (HETADI), 58–59
High-technology products (or industry), exports of, 76–77
High-technology teaching grants, 92–93
High Technology Trade Act, 77
Highways, 35
Hobbes, Thomas, 43
Housing, pension funds and, 63

Human resources
  underinvestment by the federal government in, 36
  See also Employment

Imports:
  managing, 77–78
  See also Trade
Income tax. See Tax(es)
Individual Training Account (ITA), 102–3
Industrial modernization, 14
Industry, 46–82
  agreements on modernization and growth of, 52–54
  current approach to, 49–52
  Information Revolution and, 22–23
  pension funds as source of capital for, 59–64
  research and development and, 64–66
  strategy for revitalizing, 46–49, 51–52, 79–82
  trade policy and, 69–72
  training and retraining programs of, 104–6
  vision and foresight as needs of, 79–82
Inflation, 37–39
Information Revolution, 22–23, 87
Infrastructure, deterioration and insufficient investment in, 35
Interest rates, Reagan Administration and, 28, 29
International economy, 20, 24–25
  See also Trade
Isolationism, economic, 24

Jamestown Area Labor-Management Committee, 97–98
Japan, 24, 25, 66, 67, 74, 76, 77
Job discrimination, 11
Jobs. See Employment

Job training programs, 88–89, 93–96, 100–107
Justice, 10

Kennedy, John, 15
Kissinger, Henry, 168

Labor. See Employment
Labor force
  growth of, 85
  transformation of, 23–24
Labor unions, training and retraining programs and, 106–7
Land leasing, 153

Maneuver warfare, 135–36
Marathon Oil, 50
Massachusetts Capital Resources Company, 57–58
Military, the, 13
Military doctrine, 133–36
Military equipment, 136–38
Military reform, 130–40
  bureaucracy, 138–40
  doctrine, 133–36
  equipment, 136–38
  officer training and promotion, 132–34
  personnel, 131–32
Military strategy, 126–29
Minorities, 24
Monetary policies, 27–30
MX missile, 166

Navy, British, 140
Navy, U.S., 127–29, 135–39
Norris, William, 105
Nuclear test ban, 169–70
Nuclear war, prevention of, 157–76
  anti-ballistic missile (ABM) treaty and, 169
  as central organizing principle, 164–67
  deterrence and, 159, 164
  myths concerning, 161–63
  new arms control negotiating agenda and, 170–71

Nuclear war (*Cont.*)
SALT (Strategic Arms
Limitation Talks) II treaty
and, 160, 167-70
spread of nuclear weapons
and, 172-76
Nuclear weapons, 121
control of, 122, 160-64
spread of, 162-63, 172-76

Oil imports, 122-23
discouraging, 154-55
See also Energy security,
141-56
Oil reserve, 144-45
Organization of Petroleum
Exporting Countries
(OPEC), 24, 25, 144, 145
Ortega y Gasset, José, 91

Paine, Tom, 66
Pension funds, 55, 59-64
employee participation in
investment decisions of, 61
new investment
opportunities for, 62-64
relaxing legal restrictions
on, 61-62
state investment
clearinghouses and, 62
PLATO system, 105
Protectionist policies, 68-71

Quality of work life (QWL)
movement, 112-113

Rapid Deployment Force,
143
Reagan, Ronald (Reagan
Administration), 74
budgets of, 30-33
economic policies of
(Reaganomics), 27-33, 55
education under, 87, 88
energy policy of, 142, 145,
148, 150, 153
industrial policy of, 50-51
nuclear weapons policy of,
160, 167-69, 174
Regulations. *See* Government
regulations

Research and development
(R & D), 64-66
Rogers, Will, 30, 44

Sabbaticals, 116
SALT (Strategic Arms
Limitation Talks) II
treaty, 160, 167-70
Saving-for-training system,
102-3
Savings-incentive tax, 43-45
Schweke, William, 61
70001, Limited, 96
Sloan, Alfred P., 49
Small business, 54-59
Soviet Union, 76
military power of, 122,
126-29, 135
nuclear weapons and. *See*
Nuclear war, prevention
of
State development agencies,
57-58
Strategic Petroleum Reserve,
144-45
Synthetic Fuels Corporation
(SFC), 155-156

Tax(es), 39-44
corporate, 40
fair, 42-44
flat, 41-42
for job training or
retraining program, 103-4
savings-incentive, 43-45
windfall profits, 153
Tax-based incomes policy
(TIP), 37-39
Tax code, complexity of, 39, 40
Tax cuts:
elimination of last scheduled
10 percent, 32
of Reagan Administration,
29, 32
Tax exemptions, 40-41
Tax expenditures, 34
Tax shelters, 40, 44
Technologies:
Information Revolution and,
22-23
See also Industry

Trade, 14, 25, 66-69
current trends in, 66-67
policy goals for, 71-72
promoting American
exports, 72-77
protectionist policies and,
68-71
unfair trade practices of
other nations and, 67, 69-
70
TRW company, 111-12

Unemployment, 19, 32
Unemployment insurance,
reform of, 101
Unions. *See* Labor unions
United Auto Workers, 107
Universities and colleges,
86-88
USSR. *See* Soviet Union
U.S. Steel, 50

Vaughan, Roger, 103
Venture, capital, 54-59

Wage discrimination, against
women, 107-10
Wages, tax-based incomes
policy (TIP) and, 37-39
Watergate scandal, 9-10
Water systems, 35
Weidenbaum, Murray, 31
Weinberger, Caspar, 142-43
Wells, H. G., 90
Windfall profits tax, 153
Women:
in the labor force, 23
pay equity for, 107-10
Work:
new approaches to
organization and
management of, 110-16
See also Employment
Workers. *See* Employment;
Labor; Unemployment
Work hours, flexible, 114-15

Zumwalt, Adm. Elmo R., Jr.,
139